Past Resort

A MINERVA BIGGS MYSTERY

CORDELIA ROOK

D1607851

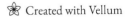

Chapter One

Highlight/lowlight of the Carolinas Gatsby League's live-action role-play event:

Violet Kilkelly was such a prime example of a high-maintenance client she was almost a caricature of one, which turned out to be a highlight, because she paid extra for me (and my dog Plantagenet along with me) to be on site and on call for the whole week. I liked my apartment just fine, but I liked Tybryd more, and who wouldn't? Even the worst guest room in the building we staff affectionately referred to as *the little inn* was a lot more luxurious than my milk-crate furniture and tea-stained throw pillows. And all the Tybryd food, no matter which building it was in, was spectacular.

As for the lowlight, that would have to be the murder.

Although the shapeless lavender housedress I was wearing to greet the guests as they arrived was a closer second than you might think. It wasn't just ugly, it was *itchy*. And hot. And light enough to show all the black dog hair I would be covered in before much longer, if I wasn't already.

The black dog in question had it much better, with nothing but a dapper gold bowtie that didn't even cramp his style. Plant was something of a dandy.

We were lined up in front of the little inn with a half dozen uniformed bellhops, like we were the staff in some gothic movie about an English country estate. The Carolinas Gatsby League had booked this more private space (officially dubbed Shining Rock Hall, despite being neither rocky nor shiny) in its entirety, as large event parties often did. In the league's case, their priority was protecting their immersion as much as possible, which made checking in at the main hotel out of the question. Much like me wearing anything remotely bearable was out of the question.

The first car to arrive was the giant white SUV Violet had told me to expect her in. "That will be Violet Kilkelly, and her husband Ray," I said to the closest bellman. "Room 416."

While he pulled Violet and Ray's luggage out of the back of the SUV, Violet hopped out of the front like the car was on fire, no doubt eager to leave the modern contraption behind. She wore an intricately beaded flapper-style dress that was way too formal for daytime, had it really been 1924. Too short for 1924 hemlines, too. I was pretty sure they'd stayed well below the knee until the latter part of the decade.

Ray clambered out of the driver's seat to join his wife, looking like he was going to a Halloween party as an old-timey gangster. He was a handsome guy, and I suspected at least a decade—maybe two—younger than his fifty-four-year-old wife, but he had none of Violet's charisma.

Which she exuded in spades. Not to mention she could easily have passed for a decade—maybe two— younger herself. Tall, ebon-haired, and porcelain-skinned, Violet looked more like a movie star than the eccentric president of a weird club, and she carried herself like a queen. Even that hop had looked regal.

She beamed at me as she took both of my hands. "Mrs. Biggs. How lovely to meet you in person at last, after so many conversations."

The *Mrs.* was not unexpected, despite my unmarried state. I'd been advised in advance that all the league's members would be arriving in character, and that to the extent reasonably possible, I should do my best to allow them to remain so at all times. Once upon a time, all housekeepers were addressed as married women, and it seemed *housekeeper* was the closest role they could come up with for the person who was to be at their beck and call at all times.

"Likewise, ma'am," I said, and wondered if I ought to curtsey or something. We staff weren't required to play our parts, only to look them, but I had the sense there would be a nice tip in it for me if I did a little bit of playing as well.

But Violet had already looked away, to flash her brilliant smile at Plant. "And so nice to see you too, little man. Or not so little. You look bigger in real life than you did on screen."

"He gets that a lot," I said. No matter how often I

used the words *big dog*, people always seemed surprised by just how big I was talking. Violet had seen Plant on our first video call, immediately declared him adorable, and insisted that since he was going to be staying with me anyway, he be present with the group as much as possible, as a sort of mascot. Her enthusiasm had never quite reached her eyes, though, and I suspected hers was more a politician's affection for dogs than a genuine one.

Plant thumped his tail against the sidewalk by way of greeting, but remained sitting. I'd already given him a strict order to *stay*, lest he make the egregious error of getting hair or drool on the esteemed founder and president of the Carolinas Gatsby League.

Violet gave him the lightest of pats on the head before turning back to me. "Everything jake?"

"Yes ma'am, everything's fiz—jake." I'd learned a little bit of twenties slang ahead of time, but the twentieth was really not my century of expertise, and I wasn't entirely comfortable with the jargon yet.

She waved at Ray. "My husband, Ray. Ray, come and meet Mrs. Biggs."

"In a moment, darling." Ray gave me a brusque nod before turning back to the bellhops, to whom he was giving copious (and entirely unnecessary) instructions for the handling of his luggage. His voice was overloud and overbearing.

I couldn't tell whether this bluster was his own, or his character's. I'd been told that for simplicity's sake, all the characters had the same names as their players—Violet was to be Violet, Ray to be Ray, etc.—but I knew nothing else about their roles. As I understood it, live-action role-play involved some sort of shared story, but I'd been given no information as to the plot of this one.

I'll admit, I was curious enough to be looking forward to doing a little eavesdropping. It was easier to grasp the sort of LARPing that involved armor and swords, or Revolutionary War reenactments; those were based in combat. There would be a mock battle, or several, and somebody would emerge a winner. But how did a person "win" a week-long Gatsby party? And what was the prize when they did?

I flicked through the envelopes in the wooden box I held, looking for the one marked Room 416. The room's keycards were inside, so as to keep the unsightly modern things out of view. I handed it to Violet, but she barely glanced at it before taking my elbow and leading me aside, almost into the shrubbery that lined the drive.

"Minerva," she said, barely above a whisper, and my heart sank. I took the use of my first name to mean she'd dropped character. Which almost certainly meant I'd done something that she felt needed correction. Already.

"Is something wrong?" I asked.

"No, no, darling, I'm sure you've done an excellent job. Only you never mentioned to me that the ferris wheel had been updated."

I blinked at her. "Updated?"

"It's not in its original condition."

"You mean ... its original condition from when it was built in 1924?" I did my best to keep my face neutral despite the laugh that was knocking at the back of my throat. "I'm sorry, I assumed you would have realized it would be modernized. It wouldn't be safe, otherwise."

She sighed, apparently disappointed by my—and Tybryd's—interest in safety. "But the wheel is so famous. I guess I expected it would be preserved, you know, like the landmark it is. Part of the reason we chose Tybryd is that Tybryd was *here* during our time." She waved at the inn behind me. "Not this particular building, maybe, but details like the ferris wheel and the hedge maze go a long way. The ferris wheel especially, because it was built in the same year our game is set."

I suppressed a sigh of my own. The little inn had been constructed in the 1990s, but it was designed to match the nineteenth-century splendor of the rest of Tybryd, right down to the signature red roof. There was a lot we could do—and had done—with decorations, food, drinks, and other temporary arrangements to give it the feel of 1924. What we could not do, as I'd repeatedly explained to Violet, was provide the Carolinas Gatsby League with an actual time machine.

But if she hadn't taken in that message the first dozen times I'd said it, I doubted I'd have any better luck now. "I'm so sorry you're disappointed," was the best I could manage.

"Well." Violet offered me another dazzling smile. "We make do with what we've got, don't we? I—" She cut herself off with an excited squeal. "*Goldie!*"

I turned to find that three more cars had pulled up while we were talking, and the front of the inn was now the site of a small crowd. The woman Violet had thrown herself at to hug was presumably her (real life) sister Marigold, known to all as Goldie. True to her name, she sported a bob so yellow that the word *blonde* didn't seem to cover it. As she pulled back from Violet, I took in her big eyes, delicate nose, and sweet smile, and felt a little bad for her; in any other family, she'd have been the beauty.

I clapped my thigh for Plant and walked over to the nearest new arrival, a slim, short older woman with a mass of gray curls. While I introduced myself, Plant made his own introduction, in the form of a wildly wiggling back end. She seemed delighted by his enthusiasm, and cooed over him as she bent to scratch his ears. Plant could always spot the dog lovers.

The woman gave her name as Maryjo, and I accordingly searched out the proper envelope and gave her her room number. As we were finishing this bit of business, we were both distracted by raised voices. I looked up to find Ray looming over a heavyset, mild-faced man.

"... best learn to control your wife!" Ray stepped even closer, until he was right in the guy's face. "Before she finds herself in hot water and then some!"

The other man shook his finger at Ray, but it looked half-hearted at best. I got the impression the red in his cheeks was more embarrassment, or maybe shyness, than anger. "Now you ... uh ... you see here, Kaminski! You'd best watch your mouth!"

"Kilkelly," Goldie stage-whispered. "His name is Kilkelly, Frank."

Poor form, Frank, I thought. *Even I knew that.* Ray was Violet's third—or maybe fourth—husband, and she hadn't taken any of their names. Since married couples having separate names wasn't really a thing in 1924, for

7

LARPing purposes both Violet and Ray were to be called by Violet's surname.

Although to be fair, if this was the quality of dialogue that could be expected of this group, I wasn't sure Frank calling somebody by the wrong name was their biggest problem.

I leaned in closer to Maryjo. "Who is Frank, in relation to everybody else?"

"Goldie's husband, in both reality and role-play. Had to be positively dragged here, poor guy. He *hates* being the center of attention." She gave me a mischievous grin that looked like it should have belonged to a young girl. "I do hope someone warned you about Goldie and Ray?"

"I was instructed not to seat them near one another." I had, in fact, been given several pairs of names that I was not to seat near one another. I assumed it was all manufactured conflict, for the role-play. It seemed unlikely that twenty-one people who belonged to what was apparently a close-knit club, who had regular meetings and spent their vacations together, could all hate one another. But *They were all good friends and enjoyed one another's company* wouldn't make for a very action-packed story.

"Oh goodness, no, *definitely* don't put them next to each other," Maryjo said. "One or both of them would be stabbed before the night was out. Goldie despises Ray. Do you know he's *seventeen years* Violet's junior?" She pursed her lips, though she seemed to be holding back a smile. "Quite the scandal. Goldie believes he only married Violet for her fortune. Which is *considerable*."

"Ahh." I tried to channel my friend Paul's most

gossipy expression, in an attempt to look interested. "And what do you think?"

"Who cares if he did?" Maryjo shrugged. "Violet gets what she wants either way, doesn't she?"

"Well, I suppose that depends on whether what she wants is real love."

She laughed and patted my arm. "Oh, my dear. Very little in Violet's life is real. I don't think she minds a bit."

That comment caught all the interest I'd been feigning up to that point. I wondered whether we were talking about Game Violet or Real Violet, and how much of this business about Ray marrying her for money and Goldie not liking it was true. But I decided it wasn't my place to ask.

Besides, Maryjo had already moved on to other topics, and other people. She was waving frantically at a pretty, petite brunette who'd just gotten out of her car. "Stasia! Stasia, darling, over here!"

Stasia came over and air-kissed both of Maryjo's cheeks before smiling at me. (Plant wagged his tail at her, but she either didn't see him, or didn't like dogs, because she ignored him.) "Mrs. Biggs, I presume?"

"You presume correctly." I found her envelope and handed it over. "You're in room 415, across the hall from Violet. She requested that you be close to one another."

"But they already *are* close to one another." Maryjo's chuckle sounded forced. And maybe a tiny bit jealous. "They're very best friends."

"Not this week." Stasia gave me a subtle wink. "At the moment, we're mortal enemies. She probably asked for my room to be close so she could whack me over the head with a lead pipe while everyone else is sleeping. I don't suppose you could change our rooms, so we're not near each other after all?"

"I ..." I bit my lip. "I'm sorry. I can't tell if that's a genuine request or not." I hadn't thought the role-play would be a big deal; what did I care if these people weren't being themselves, when I didn't know them anyway? But now that I was in the middle of it, I was finding it a little disconcerting.

"Oh, it is," said Stasia. "I won't let you get in trouble for it, I promise. I'll take full responsibility."

"Here, switch rooms with me." Maryjo handed her envelope to Stasia. "I'm on the second floor."

"Who's switching rooms?" Goldie came over to greet Stasia with a hug.

"Stasia and I." Maryjo cast an ostentatious glance around us, then lowered her voice. "It seems Stasia doesn't trust Violet Kilkelly."

"And who can blame her for that?" Judging by the weird accent Goldie was putting on, everybody seemed to be firmly back in character. If they'd ever been out of it.

"I'd have asked for her to switch anyway, if she was willing," Maryjo said. "Stasia was in 415, which adds up to ten, and ten is my very luckiest number. Whereas 213 adds up to six *and* has a thirteen in it."

Stasia rolled her eyes. "You and your numbers. You're almost as superstitious as Violet."

"Well, it's a good thing for us you're not superstitious at all, and don't mind sleeping in 213." Maryjo gave a little affected shudder. "I just hope you'll be safe in there."

"I assure you, I'll be safer there than in the other," said Stasia.

"Young lady," somebody else said. "Young *lady*!"

I'd been making a note of the room change in my appropriately low-tech paper notebook, but looked up at the pompous, disapproving masculine voice hovering closer to my ear than I would have liked. I found that it belonged to a bald, gray-bearded man with that particular sort of softness that seems to afflict people who were once athletic, but have let themselves go.

I guessed I was the young lady being summoned. "Sir?"

"I called you five times, at least." He jerked his chin at Plant. "He heard me. Maybe you should put him in charge."

If Plant had indeed noticed the man, he must have lost interest quickly, because he was paying him no mind at all now. With a yawn, he lay down at Maryjo's feet.

"I apologize, sir," I said. "May I have your name?"

"Bolozky." He spelled it for me. "First name, Stan. What floor am I on, please?"

"The third, Mr. Bolozky." I handed him his envelope, looking around at the chaos rather than at him. "I don't see any free bellhops at the moment, but as soon as one becomes available they'll see to your luggage."

"Bah." Stan Bolozky waved this away. "I can carry my own, and you can call me Stan. My real question is, what's this I hear about the ferris wheel being modernized?"

I was frankly stunned that this was an actual question that more than one person was having. After a quick cough to cover my laugh, I gave him the same explanation I'd already given Violet.

Stan accepted it even less readily, and talked to me at length about the safety mechanisms of amusement park rides, and all the ways "a guy" could make an old-fashioned ferris wheel perfectly safe to ride, if he only knew what he was doing.

I nodded until my eyes glazed over, while Goldie, Stasia, and Maryjo all drifted away to greet other friends. Nobody seemed all that eager to greet Stan, which surprised me not at all.

In the end, I was rescued by a bellman, and eventually I got all twenty-one members of the Carolinas Gatsby League checked in and sent off to their rooms. I had a little time before I had to start setting up for dinner, so I clipped on Plant's leash and took him around the back of the little inn, where there was a small pond.

"So much drama, Plant," I said as we passed the gazebo and started around the pond. "Ferris wheel drama, no less."

Plant lunged toward a heron standing at the edge of the water, possibly blaming it for the drama.

"Leave it." I yanked him back. "Imagine living the kind of life where *ferris wheel drama* is a thing. Don't these people have real problems?"

Little did I know. If they didn't, they were about to —as was I.

Chapter Two

"THEY LOOK like they're having fun." Percy squeezed my hand and smiled out over the room, which we'd converted from restaurant dining room to faux mansion dining room. The tables were pushed together to form one giant one, where all twenty-one players were presently chatting and eating (and drinking) away. With the flowers, silver candlesticks, and expensive knick-knacks we'd arranged to make the room look more homey, it wasn't all that different from his own dining room back at Baird House. The main difference being the great quantity of beaded bags and feathered fans and long cigarette holders that covered this particular table.

My return smile abruptly died as I took in Percy's gray suit. Which his broad shoulders looked amazing in, but that was not the point. "What are you *doing*?" I grabbed his arm and dragged him out the double doors whence he'd just come, then closed them softly behind me. "You can't be in there!"

He blinked at me. "I ... own the resort?"

13

I rolled my eyes. "There's no need to pull rank. You aren't dressed for it!"

"Aw, come on, the guys don't look that different. It's not like we have to wear"—he started to gesture at my dress, then his eyes widened—"What did they *do* to you?"

"Nice." I looked down at the lavender nightmare. "It's a housedress."

"It clashes with your hair."

"Nothing clashes with brown."

"It's got more red in it these days. I thought you got highlights or whatever."

"Nope. Must be getting some sun on all those hikes we've been taking. And I know how ridiculous I look, you know, there's no need to point it out."

"The *dress* looks ridiculous. *You* look beautiful, as always." Percy glanced up and down the empty hallway before giving me a kiss. We'd only been together a couple of months, and he knew I still wasn't all that comfortable with kissing the boss while I was working. "Anyway"—he gave his tie a little tug—"a suit's a suit."

"To the untrained eye, maybe. Which, to be fair, a lot of these seem to be." I gave him a scandalized look. "A couple of them are wearing *polyester*."

"I take it that's bad?"

"Not if they were doing the 40s. And the fringe! So much fringe."

"Also bad?"

"Not as bad as the polyester, but it's more Halloween flapper than historical flapper. Fringe wasn't as common as the cheap costumes would have you believe. Not that these costumes are cheap. Even the polyester ones look expensive."

Percy chuckled. "Well, as somebody who holds and participates in a costume party every year, I can't exactly judge them. It is going well, though?"

"I think so. The meal looks delicious, and I assume LARPers are like everybody else in that they vacation mostly for the food."

"Probably. Anyway, I just wanted to check in."

"Uh-huh." I pursed my lips at him. "Much like Sajani 'just wanted to check in' half an hour ago." Tybryd had never hosted a LARP event before, and everybody seemed to find the idea highly entertaining. I suspected *I wanted to check in* really meant *I wanted to check it out*.

He flashed me the dimples. "Fine, I wanted to do a little spying. Looks like it's going well."

"For the moment. But don't be trying to distract me with those dimples, I've got to get back to work."

"All right, all right. Does Plant need a walk?"

I shook my head. "He's passed out upstairs, exhausted by his hosting duties."

"I'll make sure he gets paid time and a half." Percy gave me a quick kiss goodbye. I might have watched him walk away for a little too long.

Goldie caught me doing it. As I was looking down the hall, she came up it from the direction of the restrooms. Without slowing her stride, she did a little twirl to check out Percy's retreating back, then waggled her brows at me. "Who's your fella? He's cute."

I did my best not to laugh at her affected accent, which came out more Kennedy Impersonator than East-

Egg Aristocracy. "That's Percy Baird. He and his sister own this, um, joint. He was just stopping by to make sure you guys ... uh, and gals ... you guys and gals are happy." As soon as the words left my mouth, I cursed myself inwardly for neglecting to say *guys and dolls*.

Goldie noticed my awkwardness (no surprise, since it was hard to miss) and immediately dropped the accent. "Hey, don't sweat the language on my account. I don't take this RP stuff as seriously as the rest of them. In fact, it'd be a relief to use regular words once in a while." She leaned closer and gave me a one-of-the-guys nudge on the shoulder. "This is my first one, so believe me, I totally get how insane we all look to you."

"You look nothing of the kind!" I protested. Even though they did, a tiny bit. "I just want you to enjoy yourselves."

Goldie snorted. "Oh, we'd *better* enjoy ourselves. Whether we like it or not."

I raised my brows. "Is there some sort of Gatsby police force that will give you a citation, if you don't?"

"Worse. *Vi* will give us a citation. It is especially important that Frank and I enjoy ourselves. You know, she planned this big blowout this year, having it here at Tybryd and all this fanfare, for our sakes, to impress us."

"No, I didn't know."

"Oh, yeah. I think she usually just rents a couple of cabins or something. But she finally talked us into doing it, what, maybe ten years after she started the whole thing?"

"How'd she manage that?" I asked.

Goldie shrugged. "Like she manages most things—

with sheer determination and no small amount of nagging. And who knows, maybe all this Roaring Twenties stuff is in our blood. My father used to tell us stories about the family fortune originating with a bootlegger."

"Really?" I laughed. "A real-life Gatsby."

"Who knows if it's true, Dad was a joker. Anyway, if the gene is there, it seems to have skipped me. I'm being a good sport for Vi, but I can't say I'm super into this stuff." She patted my shoulder. "So any time you need a break from playing the housekeeper, you can come talk to me. Although I bet you'd rather talk to that cute guy. Or your dog!"

Goldie looked around, as if expecting to see Plant materialize. "He didn't come to dinner?"

I shook my head. "The health code kind of frowns on dogs in restaurants."

"Even for a private event?"

"Eh." I tilted my hand back and forth. "I saw no reason to push it. Not everybody wants to see a dog at the dining table."

"Well *I* would have liked to see him. He's a beautiful dog."

I smiled. "Thank you, he is."

Goldie sighed. "I always wanted a dog. Used to beg for one when I was little. But Vi ..." She waved a hand, as if the word *Vi* explained everything.

"She didn't want one?" I asked.

"Something like that. My father didn't think she— we—could be trusted to properly care for a pet." Goldie smirked as she turned toward the restaurant doors. "He wasn't wrong. We weren't the most responsible kids in the world. Shall we?"

I opened one of the doors and stepped back for her. "After you."

She swept past me and did a little shimmy as she made her way back to her seat. Not that anybody noticed. In true Gatsby style, both the laughter and the liquor were flowing freely, and the atmosphere already seemed in some danger of tipping past *festive* and into *unruly*. At one point Maryjo, apparently taking an offhand joke of Violet's as a command, hopped up onto her chair and demonstrated her version of the Charleston. Which looked nothing like the actual Charleston. Her rhythm was understandably off, considering there was no music.

While the (costumed) restaurant manager supervised the presentation of the next course, I took a lap around the room to make sure nobody was out of sorts—or out of place. Violet had insisted on the head of the table, of course, with Ray at the foot. The seating chart was not arranged the way it would have been for an actual dinner party in 1924, but then I had a lot of restrictions to work with.

Which turned out to be a good thing. Ray's voice boomed from the other side of the room. "... knew the instant I met Vi. The very moment! Same for her, of course, with me. My wild youth has passed, boys. Shame for the ladies, but ..." He raised his glass, beaming across the long table at Violet. "I only have eyes for my beautiful wife."

Stasia made a little huffing sound into her wine glass.

PAST RESORT

Goldie snorted. "But you have *hands* to spare, from what I've seen."

Ray narrowed his eyes at Goldie. "Of course, it really helped, with that whole love at first sight business, that the first time I saw Violet was in a very flattering light. She was standing next to her sister at the time!"

The man on Ray's left burst out laughing, while the woman on his right squirmed. Frank patted Goldie's hand and murmured something to her, as if trying to calm her, but she didn't look particularly volatile. She only rolled her eyes before finishing her drink in a single swallow.

I wondered again how much of their backstory was theirs, and how much their characters'. Did Real Goldie and Real Ray actually detest each other, or was it just Game Goldie and Game Ray? Not that it mattered, beyond satisfying my curiosity. For my purposes this week, Real and Game were one and the same.

Violet caught my eye and flicked two fingers toward herself, summoning me. She waited for me to lean down into conspiracy range before whispering, "Perhaps it would be best if you suggested to your staff that Ray's drinks be watered down a bit, from here."

"Yes, ma'am." I headed toward the bar to attend to this instruction.

Or to pretend to attend to it? I hesitated, unsure whether it was a real instruction or not, then decided she must have meant it. There would be no point in role-playing if I was the only one who could hear it.

With Ray's buzz thus killed, dinner wound down without incident. The players dispersed to the duo of rooms we'd set up for their after-dinner entertainment, one as a game room and the other as a music room with a piano. Eventually, they would all end up in the little inn's small ballroom, where they would nanty-nark and generally act like West-Egg rabble-rousers until night gave way to morning.

But the night shift was more than capable of handling that without me. I fled as soon as Violet dismissed me, looking forward to a quiet hour in my room, eating taffy and reading with Plant snuggled up against my side.

It seemed I wasn't the only one to decide she'd prefer to skip both rabble and rousing. By the time I said goodnight to the restaurant staff and made my way up to the second floor, Stasia was down the hall, kneeling in front of what looked like the spilled contents of her beaded handbag, muttering to herself as she gathered it all up.

"Stupid clasp," I heard as I approached. "Stupid bag ... stupid game ... stupid men ..."

"Here, let me help you," I said.

Stasia jerked as she looked up, clearly startled.

I knelt beside her and handed her her lipstick. "Sorry, I didn't mean to sneak up on you."

"That's all right. The catch on my bag broke as I was getting my key, and everything fell out. I think that's everything now though." She stood.

"Turning in early?" I asked. "Is there anything you need?"

"No, no. I went to the game room, but I just didn't want to play, so ..." Stasia waved vaguely upward, fingers fluttering over her forehead. "I have this headache. And they're being really loud down there."

I nodded and wished her a good night. Funny though, I thought as I walked away, that *stupid headache* hadn't been on her list of stupid things. I wondered if the headache was a made-up excuse, because she didn't want to complain to a stranger about the stupid game (or the stupid men).

When I walked into my room, Plant pulled his blanket off the bed to show me, wiggling like a madman. He was always a little insecure in new surroundings. When I finally got him settled down, I at last leaned back with a pile of taffy, a bottle of water, and a book I'd been dying to finish.

Sadly, I was not to finish it that night. (Or that week, as it would turn out.) I still had thirty pages and several pieces of taffy left, when I was interrupted by a scream from downstairs.

Chapter Three

PROBABLY I WAS BEING TOO cautious. Probably it was just role-play. But that scream had unsettled even Plant, and I was happy to have him with me. I was neither big nor strong, and at the tender age of twenty-nine I'd been shot twice and attacked once. Any situation that involved screaming, I was bringing my guardian dog to.

There was no screaming now, but I did hear a raised—and outraged, by the sound—voice as I approached the game room. I walked in to find two servers and one busboy lined up in front of Violet, who appeared to be delivering a scathing lecture. There were ten or so other Gatsby Leaguers in the room, some standing, some seated at card tables, watching the show.

Plant wagged his tail at everybody, apparently under the impression that this was all a fizzing adventure. That made me feel better; if anybody had been murdered, surely he'd have smelled the blood and alerted me, right?

That seemed like the sort of thing dogs should be able to do.

Violet immediately shifted her attention to me. "*Mrs.* Biggs!" She thrust her fists against her hips.

"What seems to be the trouble, Mrs. Kilkelly?" I asked.

"My pearl-studded hair comb is gone!" Violet announced. "Someone nicked it! It must have been one of the staff. I demand you search their rooms at once."

I'd seen that comb in her hair at dinner; it looked like a true antique, and the pearls looked real. It was almost certainly valuable, and not the sort of thing I would go playing a game with, personally. But since she'd demanded I conduct a search rather than call the police or security, I could only assume this was staged.

Which was, frankly, pretty annoying. I didn't mind staying on site to manage their event. I didn't even mind playing along, a little bit and occasionally. But that didn't mean I wanted to be part of the drama. Especially after hours. And the rest of the staff definitely hadn't signed up for this.

Besides, the guests were all here to play, and they were paying a pretty price for it. Why couldn't she have picked one of her own club to accuse or make demands of?

"Odsbodikins," I muttered under my breath.

"Pardon me, dear?" Violet arched a brow at me. She wouldn't have known that Victorian slang was just a regular thing for me; she probably thought I'd gotten my eras confused. Or maybe she didn't even realize it was the wrong era, and thought I was doing an extra good job. "I didn't quite catch that."

Rather than answer her, I cast an apologetic glance at the three beleaguered staff members, all of whom looked like they were halfway to quitting. "Thank you. You guys can go."

"What do you mean, they can go?" Violet huffed. "You aren't even going to search their rooms?"

"Mrs. Kilkelly, the staff don't have rooms," I said. "They work in shifts, and come and go between here and their homes, which are mostly in Bryd Hollow. Apart from the guests, I'm the only one with a room right now."

"Well then, you ought to search their pockets!" Violet demanded.

"Yes, indeed!" Ray stepped up beside his wife, looking twice as outraged as she did. "See here, we won't tolerate this! We won't go to bed until it's found!"

The servers and busboy hastened their departure. I stared at Violet and Ray. Just how far were they thinking I would go for their little game of pretend? "Searching the staff will not be possible."

By the look on Ray's face, I was pretty sure I wasn't going to like whatever it was he started to say in reply, so I cut him off. Which was probably a little unprofessional, but there was a line, and patting people down without their consent was for sure over it. "Why don't we start at the beginning, Mrs. Kilkelly? Where did you see the comb last?"

Violet shook her glossy waterfall of hair, maybe to demonstrate that the comb was not, in fact, in it. "I took it out at the table over there." She waved vaguely behind her. "It was pinching me."

"And who were you sitting with?"

"Mitch, Stan, and Maryjo."

Suppressing a sigh over somehow getting sucked into this, I craned my neck to look behind her. Maryjo had taken the nearest chair, elbow on the table and hand propping up her forehead, eyes half closed. Either she had a headache, or she was tired. Or tired of Violet's antics. Or all three. I noticed Plant had gone over to her. He offered her a couple of kisses before lying under the table, half on her feet.

Stan sat beside Maryjo, arms folded across his barrel chest. I guessed the know-it-all I'd met earlier was out of character for the Stan he was playing now, because he looked like he was (somewhat painfully, by his face) holding back a lecture of his own. No doubt Violet wouldn't have tolerated the competition.

I rifled through my memory until I found an image of Mitch, the final player at Violet's table. Big. Buzz cut. Looked like a boxer. He was nowhere to be seen. "Where is Mitch now?" I asked.

Ray's eyes flicked to me, then away. "He went to bed."

"He was zozzled," Maryjo added, which I took to mean drunk.

For a second, I felt a little flare of hope. Maybe the obvious answer would get me back to my book. And my taffy. "Could he have taken the comb with him? Maybe he picked it up by accident."

"Oh, I doubt that," said Maryjo. "He wasn't at the table anymore, when he left."

Still a *no* on that taffy, then. "All right, where was he when he left?"

"Across the room." Maryjo waved in the general direction of the window. "Punching Ray in the kisser."

"Stomach." Ray glowered at Maryjo, then at Violet, although the latter hadn't said a word. "He punched me in the stomach."

I crossed my arms. It was late, I was tired, and they were wasting time burying the lede? "It would be easier if you told me the whole story at once, rather than doling it out bit by bit like this."

"I'll tell it, as an objective witness," Goldie offered.

"Objective my eye," Ray muttered.

Goldie ignored him, which was a relief. Squabbling would only make this take longer. "We were all playing cards. Vi and Mitch were at this table"—she rapped her knuckles against the table in question—"Ray was at that one"—she pointed—"and I was here." She walked to another table and tapped the back of a chair. "With Frank, Clarice, and Kirk. So we had a good view of the action. They'll correct me if I get anything wrong, right you guys?"

The *you guys* was probably not on point for the role-play, but nobody corrected her. Her three partners-in-cards nodded. Goldie turned back to me. "Ray heard Mitch say something to Vi that he—Ray—didn't like. Something suggestive. Ray is awfully jealous, for a guy with his own wandering eye."

"It wasn't exactly an isolated incident," Stan cut in. "Ray and Mitch were going at it from the second we got in the room. The very second, in fact, because Ray didn't like how Mitch was touching his wife, as they were walking in."

"Piffle." Violet rolled her eyes. "He was barely touching me at all. His hand grazed my shoulder."

"Didn't look like your shoulder to me," Stan said with a shrug.

"So anyway." Goldie's words were loud enough to carry over the others, for which I was grateful. Ray's jealousy was not the matter at hand. "Ray and Mitch started exchanging words. Next thing you know, Mitch is running over to Ray's table and punching him. Ray shoved him back. There was a little scuffle."

"How did it end?" I asked.

"Vi went to break it up," said Goldie, "then she yelled at Ray a while, and he yelled back. Somewhere along the way, Mitch stormed out of the room."

"And when I got back to my table, the comb was gone," said Violet.

"Then Mitch could have taken it," I said, "while you were occupied with Ray."

Violet huffed. "What would Mitch want with a hair comb?"

"Mitch's hair has gotten *very* thin," said Maryjo.

I tossed my hands. "I doubt whoever took it did so to use it. It's valuable, right?"

Violet gave me an impatient look. "Mrs. Biggs, I believe you are being distracted by the wrong things."

Okay, so I was playing the game wrong. They didn't want me focused on Mitch.

Yet they'd considered conducting an illegal search of Tybryd employees to be a good use of time? "Were the servers even in here, in between the last time you saw the comb, and when you noticed it was gone?"

I doubted it; if the staff had seen an actual physical fight, they would have called security. The LARP wasn't, to my knowledge, supposed to involve violence.

"I don't remember," Violet said. "They've been in and out, bringing us drinks and picking up glasses."

"And picking up hair combs, possibly," Stan added.

"It seems like anybody could have taken it, during the commotion," I said. "We could ask everybody to turn out their pockets, or something?"

Was that what I was supposed to do? Surely they wanted the attention shifted back to them. Maybe accusing the staff had just been a simple way to force my involvement. Something I continued to resent, I might add. Why couldn't one of them have role-played a famous detective?

"Has anybody else left, since you noticed the comb was missing?" I asked.

Violet bit her lip, considering this, then shook her head. "Stasia left before I took it out, I think."

I nodded. "She left really early, I saw her upstairs."

"Well, one more is leaving now." Maryjo got up. "I'm sorry, but this headache just won't go away. The aspirin did nothing for it at all."

I resisted the urge to mention that headaches seemed to be going around tonight. Maryjo stepped in front of me and opened her small clutch bag. A lipstick and her room keycard were the only things inside. "I haven't got any pockets," she said.

Close up like this, her face looked pinched and

drawn. Either she really did have a headache, or she was doing a much better acting job than the members of the Carolinas Gatsby League were, in my short experience, generally capable of. "Thank you," I said. "Have a good rest."

That seemed to be the seal that needed breaking; as soon as Maryjo left, the others started lining up and doing much the same thing, showing me the contents of their bags and pockets, then taking their leave, either for the ballroom or their beds. The comb never turned up.

Finally, with parting sneers at Ray, Goldie and Frank made their exit, leaving me alone with Violet and Ray.

I looked around the room. Tables, half-finished drinks, decks of cards. A fireplace, period-appropriate knick-knacks on the mantel. A wine-colored cloche hat somebody had left behind. One very large black dog, flat on his side and snoring under the closest table.

Not a whole lot of places to hide a jeweled hair comb, that I could see.

I narrowed my eyes at Violet. "Have you had it this whole time?"

She pressed a hand to her chest. "Had what? My comb?"

Ray laughed. "Are you suggesting she stole her own property? Why would she do such a thing?"

I put my hands on my hips. "Gosh, I don't know, maybe for drama?"

Violet pouted at me, looking irritated.

I decided I'd best nip this whole thing in the bud, lest I end up doing this every night. "Look. We're doing our best, where possible, not to break your immersion. And I think you'll agree we've done an excellent job with that, barring a few unavoidable things, and you can't really consider modern plumbing a downside, can you? But it's really not possible for us to *participate* so heavily in—"

"You think I *planned* this?" Violet's voice was just a touch less throaty, the words coming just a touch faster, and I understood she'd dropped her role.

"You didn't, then?" I asked.

"Of course not."

"So somebody actually stole your comb?" I frowned. "Why didn't you tell me to call the police?"

"Oh, no." Violet gave me a sweet smile. I assumed it was the one she generally used to placate underlings she'd riled up. "I doubt someone stole it with the intent to *keep* it, outside their role. I'm sure it's part of the RP, and they'll give it back at the end."

"But you didn't expect it," I said. "This isn't a mystery plot you've got going here?"

She shook her head. "No, not particularly."

"More of a thriller, if you want to give it a genre," said Ray, in a much milder tone than I'd heard him use before. The arrogance was gone from his face, too, and I guessed I was meeting the real Ray for the first time. "It's actually an organized-crime plot. You know, bootlegging, bosses, competing outfits. Crime outfits, I mean, not fashion." His boisterous laugh at his own joke was the same, though. "Infiltration, treachery, heartbreak. Someone is going to emerge with control of the Carolinas gin trade."

"Sounds fun," I said, not because it did, but because he looked excited, and seemed to require a response.

"But it's not like I've written scripts for people," said Violet. "How could I play too, if I did? I don't know what's going to happen any more than they do. I had no idea someone was going to steal my comb. What you saw tonight, how I responded, was just a little improvisation."

"We're all improvising, really, all the time. That's what role-playing is." Ray offered me a conciliatory look, half smile, half grimace. He wasn't as charming as his wife, but he was certainly preferable to Game Ray. "But we can try to involve you less, in the future."

"I'm more concerned that you not involve the rest of the staff at all," I said. I'd thought this was already clear, until I found them being subjected to Violet's accusations. I couldn't have the players denouncing random bartenders and maids, demanding to search people's purses. "They're willing to dress their parts, but they're still modern-day servers and such. Which means they need to be treated as serv*ers*. Not serv*ants*."

"And they need to be tipped," Violet said with a light laugh. "I promise, I've been slipping them discreet bills here and there. Your staff is being treated quite well."

I nodded. "I appreciate that."

"And we'll keep you out of it, too, from now on." Ray held out his hand, as if we were making a deal. He waited for me to shake on it, then said, "You have my word."

It was not a promise Ray would be able to keep.

Chapter Four

THE CAROLINAS GATSBY LEAGUE was running me ragged.

A large contingent went to ride the ferris wheel, the morning after they arrived, but came back in a huff when they discovered it was infested with regular hotel guests wearing jeans and shorts and walking around with smartphones. Whereupon a dozen or so of them decided to have a picnic in the rose garden instead. I didn't blame them for wanting to be outside on such a glorious late-May day, with Tybryd's gardens in bloom under the Carolina blue sky. But visiting what was easily the most popular of those gardens struck me as a spectacularly bad idea, if they wanted to avoid modern people. I suspected there would be a second huffy return before long. Nevertheless, I set about organizing baskets and searching out blankets.

Meanwhile, Violet, Ray, Stasia, and Goldie wanted high tea out on the gazebo (except at noon, in lieu of lunch, rather than at actual tea time). Mitch, Stan, and

Maryjo overheard them asking for it, declared that a splendid idea, and said they would join them. What high tea, or any of the rest of this, had to do with organized crime and the gin trade was beyond me, but it wasn't for me to judge.

I was in the middle of making all these arrangements when I felt my phone vibrate in the pocket of my shapeless housekeeper's uniform (light blue today, which was at least an improvement). Since I was in the hallway between the kitchen and the dining room at the time, and there were no LARPers there to be offended, I pulled it out and checked the screen.

Snick. That wouldn't do at all. The Bairds' household manager (I'd learned that this was a title rich people gave their butlers when they didn't want to sound snooty enough to have a butler) was a good friend of mine, and I loved talking to him. But those talks did tend to run a tad long.

I touched the green button and immediately said, "This isn't a good time," in lieu of a proper greeting.

I heard his breathy chuckle, the one he used when my suffering, or at least the anticipation of my suffering, was amusing him. "Bet it'd be an even worse time if I were asking for stuff. Which you know is what Tristan's going to do. I just called to warn you he's on his way over."

"Tristan ... Baird?" Obviously it was Tristan Baird. What other Tristan's whereabouts would Snick be privy to? But I hadn't even realized Tristan was in town. His sister Elaine's wedding—which I was planning—was still two weeks away. "When did he get here?"

"Showed up last night. I don't think anyone was

expecting him until next weekend, if you're wondering why Percy didn't tell you."

I shook my head, still confused. "And he's on his way here why?"

"He didn't give me any specifics, just asked where he could find you and said he had 'top-secret wedding business' he needed to talk to you about."

"Well, he won't find me at the events office. I'm at the little inn with the flappers this week."

"Trust me, we all remember. Percy's been going on and on about the Gatsby League and what an amazing job you've done planning their little LARP thing."

I snorted. "I wouldn't call it *little*. They're as high maintenance as they come. So you told him to come here?"

"Yep."

I groaned inwardly. It wasn't that I didn't want to see Tristan. I liked him. But I'd meant it when I said this wasn't a good time. "I don't know if I can really—"

As if to confirm that I definitely couldn't, Goldie burst through the swinging door from the dining room, looking harried. "There you are, Mrs. Biggs!"

Odsbodikins, had she heard me call the Gatsby League high maintenance? "Snick, I have to go. Thanks for the heads up."

I ended the call and held my phone behind my back, like a child hiding a stolen cookie. I wasn't supposed to allow modern gadgets to get in the players' line of sight, if I could help it. "I'm sorry, Mrs. Barillo."

She laughed. "No need to apologize. I'll tell you a secret, I've been carrying my own phone this whole time.

I even snuck a few pictures with it during dinner last night."

I already knew she had a phone; she'd shown me the contents of her handbag the night before, and it had been tucked in there. Several of the role-players, in fact, had been carrying phones. I assumed they didn't want to be so immersed as to be unreachable in the event of an emergency. But *having* phones wasn't the same as *seeing* phones. "Nobody noticed you taking pictures?"

"If they did, they chose to ignore it. Probably because they'll want to post those pictures when we get back. Anyway, it seems we're missing a picnic basket. I volunteered to look into the matter."

"I thought you were staying back for tea?"

"I am, but I'm trying to help get Frank out the door." Goldie held her hand to one side of her mouth and whispered, "He's driving me crazy."

The Mystery of the Missing Basket left me no time to wonder over (or dread) Tristan's visit. When I finished attending to the picnickers and saw them off at last, a passing server on her way out to the gazebo tea told me somebody was waiting for me in the sitting room that served as the little inn's lobby.

This turned out to be a slightly inaccurate report; when I walked into the room I found not one somebody, but two. Sitting beside Tristan in one of the plush armchairs grouped around a low table was a woman with his dark hair and thick brows. She smiled in response to my greeting, and there were Percy's dimples. A cousin, maybe?

She didn't get up, but Tristan did. He gave me a hug

and kissed both my cheeks before turning back to the woman. "So this is Minerva. Don't call her Minnie, she hates it." He looked at me as he resumed his seat. "My sister, Gwen."

My jaw dropped, and for a second I could only stammer. Gwen's family didn't speak to her. Gwen's family didn't speak *of* her. What was she doing here?

She might have had Percy's dimples, but her smile had all of Tristan's snark. "I see my reputation as the prodigal daughter has preceded me."

Tristan cocked his head at her. "Mm, I'd say you're more the wayward daughter. The prodigal son gets forgiven, right?"

Gwen raised a brow. "You don't think I'll be forgiven?"

"No one that matters thinks there's anything to forgive, so there's that." Tristan looked back at me. "Sorry, we've shocked you."

Noting the sparkle in his eye, I pursed my lips at him. "You're not one bit sorry. You're delighted to have shocked me."

Ever the pot-stirrer, that one. He grinned. "Guilty. My plan is to spring her on everyone like this. I got her a room at Tybryd under a fake name and everything. And then checked her in after I made sure Percy was gone for the day. *Super* cold-war-spy-movie stuff."

I looked from Tristan to Gwen. "So nobody knows you're here?"

Her expression was only slightly less mischievous than her brother's. "No, I want to surprise Elaine. That's why we're here, we were hoping you could help."

"I ... see." Except I didn't. I was not enjoying this nearly as much as they were. Nor did I understand how they could be enjoying it as much as they were. I knew that Gwen's grievance was with her parents, not her siblings, but still. She hadn't been home in years. Not even for her own father's funeral. Elaine and Percy might be glad to see her—maybe—but I had no idea how Mrs. B would react. And *extra drama* wasn't exactly high on my wedding planner's wish list.

I dropped into the nearest chair. "Can I get you anything? Coffee, or ...?" *Maybe a suit of armor, for when your mother finds out about this?*

"No, no," said Tristan, "we won't keep you long. We heard you're super busy with your larf. Is it larf? Lard?"

"LARP," I corrected. "It's an acronym, for live-action role-play."

Tristan nodded, although judging by the look of polite bare-interest on his face, I doubted he would retain this information. "Perce says you've been doing a bang-up job with it."

"Well, Percy's always generous with his praise."

"Really?" Gwen snickered. "That's never been my experience with him. But then he was what?" She looked at Tristan. "Nineteen the last time I saw him?"

Tristan shrugged. "Something like that."

"Not an age where boys are known for their cheerful-ness, anyway." Gwen smiled at me. "Glad to hear he's treating you guys right, though."

Possibly prompted by his sister's use of the plural, Tristan cast a look around the room. "Where's Plant? I was hoping to see him. I actually considered bringing my four today, you know how they love him. But I decided I had my hands full enough with Gwen. And *she* won't even tolerate a leash."

Tristan had four French bulldogs who did indeed love Plant, but I was glad he hadn't brought them. I felt like I had my hands full enough, myself. "Plant's napping up in my room. He's used to sleeping in the events office all day, so he's finding all the running around I've been doing exhausting."

"Oh right, right." Tristan fluttered a hand. "Super busy. Back to the subject at hand, then."

"We hear Elaine's not having a bachelorette party," said Gwen.

"No, she's not," I said. "They decided against having a wedding party, so a lot of the stuff the best man and maid of honor take on just sort of fell by the wayside."

Gwen's face fell. "I wonder if the wedding party thing is partly because of me. Because you'd usually have your sister as your maid of honor, you know?" She picked at the hem of her silk shirt. "That's why I came, I wanted to be here for her. I'm the only sister she's got, and brothers aren't the same."

I had a sneaking suspicion she was right about why Elaine didn't want a maid of honor—especially since she didn't seem to have any close girlfriends to step in—but I tried to look noncommittal. "I think they just wanted something more low key overall. Phil's a pretty laid-back guy."

Gwen still looked sad, but Tristan jumped into the awkward silence that followed. "So anyway, we thought that might be a good way to surprise Elaine. Like a surprise bachelor/bachelorette party, and we get her there, and Gwen's there. We wanted to see if you could help us plan it."

"When were you thinking?" I asked.

"Tomorrow, if not tonight," said Gwen. "I haven't been back to Bryd Hollow in a really long time. Or on vacation without my kids in a really long time, if we're being honest. I don't want to waste too much time hiding in my room, but we don't want anyone else to find out I'm here before Elaine does. So ideally, Elaine will find out quickly."

I got more and more uncomfortable with every word she spoke—for several reasons. I took a deep breath. "Okay, first of all, I'm so sorry, but there's no way I can plan a party on such short notice, with everything else I have going on. Secondly ..." I bit my lip, looking from Gwen to Tristan. "You don't mean that you expect me to keep this from Percy, right? Because that feels wrong. And I don't want to be in the middle of this."

Tristan laughed. "What, because he's your boss?" He waved a hand and went on before I could answer. "You don't have to *lie*, just don't tell him. Surely you can avoid him for one day. You don't even report directly to him, do you?"

I gaped at him. *My boss?* Suddenly Gwen saying she was glad Percy treated *us guys* right made sense—she'd been referring to Tybryd employees.

Percy hadn't told them we were together. Well, of course he hadn't told Gwen. He wasn't in touch with Gwen. But he was in touch with Tristan.

Tristan studied my face through narrowed eyes, then

39

sucked his breath through his teeth. "Ohhhh boy, I just got him in trouble, didn't I?" He wagged his finger back and forth, as if between me and an invisible Percy beside me. "You two are ..."

I cleared my throat. "Yep."

"And you expected me to know."

"Yep."

There was no good reason for me to feel hurt by this. It wasn't like I'd told my sister or my parents that I was seeing somebody. The only reason the rest of Percy's family knew was that we all lived in the same town. He and I hadn't been together very long. The only important *L* word we'd exchanged was *lunch*.

But I was irritated, just the same.

With all his usual sensitivity, Tristan burst out laughing. "And how did my mother take this?"

I shrugged. "Great, actually. You know your mom. She's happy about everything."

"Not always," Gwen muttered. "So if you're Percy's girlfriend, I can see how that complicates the whole surprise situation." She looked at Tristan, tapping her finger against her chin. "What do you say we scrap the big party idea and just, like, see if the private room at Rapunzel's is available for dinner?"

Tristan scoffed. "On a Saturday night?"

"At the house, then," Gwen said. "Assuming Mrs. B won't kick me out." I remembered Mrs. B telling me that even some of her children called her that, but it was still strange to hear it in action.

"Mom will be crying tears of joy," Tristan assured her.

Gwen clapped her hands against her thighs. "There you go then, done. Ask Dante to make something special, and I'll just show up. And see if you can get Phil to come. I want to have a look at him."

She smiled at me as she stood up. "I give you my blessing to tell Percy, but only if you swear him to secrecy. I still want it to be a surprise for Elaine. Can you make it tonight?"

"Thank you for the offer, but I have to work." I did not add that I had no desire to be there. I'd suffered through uncomfortable dinners at Baird House before, and was in no rush to repeat the experience.

"Well then, it turns out to be a good thing we came," Gwen said as I led her and Tristan back to the little inn's entrance. "I got to meet you."

"It was nice to meet you as well," I said, "and I hope we'll get a chance to spend more time together before you go. For now though, I guess I'd better get outside and see how tea is going."

"Tea?" Tristan asked. "Are they doing an Austen thing, too? I thought it was a Fitzgerald thing."

"It is, but for some reason they decided high tea was something bootleggers did." I shrugged. "I guess they—"

As I was talking, we stepped outside—and heard a chorus of shrieks from the direction of the pond. Gwen looked alarmed, but I just rolled my eyes.

"It's probably just another fake theft," I said. I wouldn't bother going to get Plant this time; I'd learned my lesson about taking the players' drama and hysterics seriously, no matter how dramatic and hysterical they might be.

Which in this case was very. The screaming, if anything, was only getting louder. Gwen and Tristan, apparently as fascinated by the idea of live-action role-play as everybody else, followed me out to the gazebo, where three little tables were laid out with tiered tea trays.

But nobody was sitting at them. Half a dozen people were huddled together, some standing, some kneeling, all yelling at one another and staring down at something between them.

Ray was shouting incoherently at everybody, looking very much like he was on the verge of collapse.

Goldie was on her phone. A smartphone, in plain view. Not a good sign.

My heart started to pound. I saw tears streaming down Goldie's face as she spoke to whomever she'd called, but I couldn't make out her words above the rest of the noise.

"Folks!" I called. "Hey! What is going on?"

None of them paid me any mind, so I did what anybody would have done in that situation: I pushed my way through them, to see what they were looking at.

Then immediately wished I hadn't. Violet Kilkelly lay on the gazebo's wooden floor.

And she was very definitely not playing dead.

Chapter Five

"I KILLED HER!" Stasia wailed, straight into Ruby Walker's face. "But I didn't *kill* her!" I'd lost count of the number of times she'd declared that she did—but also did not—kill Violet, but this last one was the first since Ruby's arrival.

Ruby took it in stride, as she did most things. She'd brought two other officers with her, which was a lot, by Bryd Hollow standards. From what I'd seen in the short time I'd lived in town, they barely had enough to keep the police station manned, and while they must have had some division between the patrol and investigative departments, that line was transparent to me. Even Ruby wore a uniform most of the time. She seemed to handle most serious things herself.

A fresh burst of sobs from behind me told me that Ray had been set off again. He stood alone at the edge of the pond, shaking and weeping, his face pale. Goldie knelt in the tall grass a few feet away, equally pale, face tear-stained but stoic now. The others who'd been at tea

—Stan, Maryjo, and Mitch—were gathered around the police officers, all talking and shouting at once.

I tried not to look in the direction of the gazebo, where I could see one of Violet's perfectly manicured hands reaching out from the shade of one of the pillars.

"Min—*Gwen*? What the ..."

I turned to see Percy, frozen in his tracks, staring open-mouthed at his sister. But before she could say anything, he shook his head as if to clear it, then hurried over to me.

He pulled me into a tight hug. I buried my face in his neck and breathed in his soapy scent, letting it soothe me, if only a little. "Your sister's here," I said. My voice sounded thick, and it was only then that I realized how close to tears I was.

I felt the rumble of Percy's chuckle against my cheek. "So I see."

"And also one of the LARPers died."

"So I heard." He pulled back, hands on my shoulders, to examine my face. "Are you okay?"

"Yeah, I'm ... I'll be fine. Shocked, I guess."

"What can I do?"

"Actually ..." I pulled my room keycard from the pocket of that stupid shapeless dress. "Can you get Plant? Maybe take him for a quick walk"—I gestured vaguely toward the little inn—"on the other side of the building, I guess. I think I'm not supposed to leave until one of Ruby's people talks to me, but he's going to have to go out pretty soon."

"Yeah, of course." Percy squeezed my hand as he took

the key. "How urgent is it, though? I don't want to leave you here."

"They'll probably kick you out anyway," Tristan said. I hadn't even noticed him and Gwen approaching, but they were standing beside me now. Tristan didn't look especially shaken. "They don't want anyone tampering with their witnesses."

Percy raised a brow at him. "I don't think 'witness tampering' means what you think it means. Somebody just died at my hotel, I think I'm okay to talk to the police about it."

If Tristan had feelings about his brother using the word *my* in relation to their celebrated ancestral home, he didn't show them. He just waved Percy's words away. "Well, I don't know all the official jargon, but on TV they're always pushing people back. You can't just walk up to where the police are, unless you were already there when they got there. I'm pretty sure that's the rule."

"I'm pretty sure you're full of—" Percy began, but Gwen cut him off.

"Don't worry." She sounded as calm as Tristan looked. But then, neither of them had seen the body. "We'll make sure Minerva's okay."

"Minerva is right here," I pointed out. "And Minerva is fine."

"I guess, if you consider talking about yourself in the third person *fine*," Tristan said.

I knew he was trying to lighten the mood—laughing in the face of tragedy was a standard Baird coping technique—but I ignored him in favor of reassuring Percy again. "I'm really fine. You'd better get Plant before he pees in your building."

In typical Percy Baird Perpetual Motion, he simultaneously rubbed the back of his neck, stuffed his other hand into his pocket, and rocked back slightly on his heels. I wondered if *he* was okay. He'd just seen his big sister for the first time in over a decade, and he hadn't even had a chance to process that, much less the whole scene around us. "I guess I could walk him quick and then come right back ..."

"Minerva?" Ruby called to me.

"Thank you." I squeezed Percy's arm, turned away, then decided PDA with one's boss became acceptable under harrowing circumstances, and turned back again to give him a parting kiss.

"I didn't *kill* her!" Stasia cried again, as I approached the knot of LARPers Ruby stood in the center of. As far as I could tell, Stasia had been the only one sitting with Violet at tea, so I could only assume the whole killing-but-not-killing thing had something to do with the game.

"You'd better back everybody up," Stan said to Ruby. Or maybe *ordered Ruby* would be a better description. "This is how a crime scene gets compromised."

Fool, I thought. Ruby wasn't an especially young woman, but she was a striking one; her cheekbones might have been sculpted by an artist, and her warm brown skin was still flawless, whatever her age. I mention her looks because Stan struck me as the sort of man who automatically dismissed beautiful women. Except he probably called them "gals."

Ruby tapped her signature teal-framed glasses down

the bridge of her nose, and regarded him from over the top of them. Any Bryd Hollow citizen would have understood what that meant, but Stan didn't know enough to be put in his place by it. "Thank you for your input, Mr. ...?"

"Bolozky." He started to spell it, but Ruby had already turned to me.

"As I was about to say, is there an out-of-the-way room big enough to keep everybody in for now? The other guests too, if they should come back. Somewhere besides the restaurant."

I nodded. "The ballroom."

"Good. I've also got some support from the county sheriff on the way, to help us get this done faster. I'll need your consent to search the building."

"Why?" Mitch demanded. "Are you looking for poison? Because she ... that was ..." He broke off with a huff, as if somebody had argued with him. "Well, it sure didn't look natural."

"It wasn't natural," said Stan, with a firm shake of his head. "That's why we're talking about a crime scene."

"A *potential* crime scene. The medical examiner"— Ruby arched a brow at Stan—"and only the medical examiner, will be determining the cause of death. But in the meanwhile, it's best if we have a look around while the scene is still fresh."

"But nobody would *poison* Violet!" said Maryjo, sounding a little stuffy from all the sobbing she'd been doing. "This must have been a ... an aneurysm, or something."

Ruby didn't comment on that, only turned back to

47

me. "Where do you keep pesticides, cleaning supplies, things like that?"

"In the basement," I said. "And yes, of course, whatever searches you need to do."

"What else is down there?" she asked.

"Um ... laundry. Storage. A really nice staff room. There's a pool table." I cringed inwardly at my own babbling. *Good job, Minerva. Because the quality of the staff room is what's important right now.*

"So there are no guest services on that floor?" Ruby asked. "No guest access?"

"None," I said. "You have to swipe a card to get the elevator to go down there, and there's a dedicated staircase off the kitchen."

His eyes on Ruby, Stan jerked his head in my direction. "She can't give you permission to search our rooms, you know. You'd need a warrant to search those. By law, we have an expectation of privacy. Hotel management can enter a room without the guest's permission, but only for certain reasons, and they *can't* ever give the police permission to search it."

Interesting, I thought, that Stan knew all of this. Was it only in that way that he knew—or "knew"—a lot of things, purely for the joy of explaining them to others? Or did he, in this case, have a specific reason to know it?

Ruby gave him the over-the-glasses look again. "Unless we have reason to believe crucial evidence is being destroyed. I notice you left that part out." Stan started to say something, but she wisely made sure he didn't get the chance, raising her voice only slightly as she went on, "Quickest and easiest thing is for you to consent to a search, if we ask you to. But of course that's up to each of you."

Without waiting for an answer, she waved the lanky, ginger-haired Roark McGinty over to us. He gave me a nod and a tight smile as he approached. It seemed meant to be bracing. How bad did I look, that everybody was so concerned I was going to break down?

"Ma'am?" he said to Ruby.

"Minerva's going to show you to the ballroom. I need everyone to stay in there until I dismiss them. Minerva, that includes you and Tristan, too, and ..." Ruby pushed her glasses back up to study Gwen, who stood where I'd left her, talking to Tristan. Percy was gone. "Is that Gwen Baird?"

"It is," I said. "She's in town for Elaine's wedding. She and Tristan were here to see me."

"Hmph." Ruby pressed her lips together. "I haven't seen her in years. Almost didn't recognize her. Her too, then. And all the staff who are present. Roark, get statements from everyone."

"Listen up, everyone!" Stan called, before either Ruby or Roark had the chance. He clapped his hands sharply. I was kind of surprised he didn't wear a whistle around his neck, for just such an occasion. "We're moving into the ballroom. Everybody comes, nobody leaves, got it?"

Ruby gave him an impatient look and added, "Officer McGinty is going to take your witness statements."

We started toward the inn, Ray leaning on Maryjo, the rest of the Gatsby Leaguers in a clump, with Tristan and Gwen at the back. I touched Roark's elbow. "Hey, would it be okay if some of the kitchen staff stayed in there for a little bit? I just want to see if they'll make some coffee."

Behind me, Mitch snorted. "I'm not drinking anything that comes out of that kitchen."

I shot him a glare over my shoulder, but decided it was a bad time to scold him.

Roark gave me an apologetic look. "Sorry, but we can't have anything in the kitchen washed or tampered with until we've had a chance to process it. I'll need the staff out of there."

Stasia was jostled into me as everybody squeezed through the front entrance. She didn't seem to notice. "I killed her," she muttered, I was pretty sure to herself. "But I didn't kill her."

"Why do you keep saying that?" Mitch demanded. "Because so help me, if you did kill her—"

"This is obviously a very difficult situation," Roark interrupted, loudly enough for the whole group to hear. "And I'm sorry for that, but it will be easier on all of us if you remain calm and orderly. Ma'am," he added to Stasia, "you might want to save your comments for your statement to me."

I went to round up the staff, and found most of them gathered in a clump in the restaurant, speculating as to what was going on. By the time I told them everything I knew (which wasn't much) and brought them to the ballroom, most of the LARPers—witnesses, now—were together at one of the larger tables around the perimeter. Stasia sat at a smaller one with Roark, who was speaking to her in a low voice. Gwen and Tristan were the only ones standing, huddled against the wall apart from everybody else, whispering to each other.

I looked around at the six members of the Carolinas Gatsby League who had not died at tea today: Stasia, shaking her head at something Roark had just said. Ray, still crying softly to himself. Mitch, still shooting murderous looks at Stasia. Goldie, shooting murderous looks at Ray. Maryjo, looking broken-hearted and afraid. Stan, looking pompous.

Maryjo's aneurysm theory seemed like a lot of wishful thinking. Heaven knew Stan and Mitch were no experts, but Ruby was. And no matter what she could (or couldn't) say out loud, her actions didn't exactly scream *natural causes, nothing to see here, move along with your day*.

Nor did I believe that any of the kitchen staff would have poisoned Violet; they weren't even the same ones she'd harassed the night before. And Tristan and Gwen certainly hadn't done it. Which left these six of Violet's closest friends and family.

I was looking at a murderer. I just didn't know which face.

Chapter Six

I stood between Tristan and Gwen, leaning against the wall while I waited for my turn to speak with Roark. The little inn staff members sat at a couple of tables nearby, murmuring to each other.

"I don't mean to be insensitive," Gwen said to me, "but do you have any idea how long this will take? Now that Percy's seen me, I'd really like to talk to him."

I wondered whether that feeling was mutual. I'd never heard Percy say a bad thing about Gwen, but that was partly because I'd never heard him say any kind of thing about Gwen. "No idea," I said, "but I imagine Percy will come and find us when he's finished with Plant."

"Plant's your dog, right?" Gwen waited for my nod and said, "Interesting name for a dog."

"It's short for Plantagenet."

She made a breathy sound that might have been a chuckle. "Is that meant to make it less weird?"

"Why isn't he doing us first?" Tristan tossed his head

at Roark. "We don't have much to say, and then we could get out of here."

I shrugged. My guess was that Roark would rather get statements from the ones who did have things to offer first, while the details were still fresh in their minds.

Or maybe he just thought it was most efficient to go straight to the one who kept screaming that she'd killed the victim.

All of the guests' eyes were on Stasia and Roark. Judging by his tone of voice and the way he leaned in front of her, blocking her from the others' view, Roark was trying to have a semi-private conversation. But Stasia spoke loudly enough for everybody to hear, and I had the sense it was on purpose.

"My *character* poisoned her," she said, her voice thick with tears. "It was *pretend*. It was a *game*!" She reached into her handbag and pulled out a small brown bottle. "See, cyanide smells like almonds, did you know that?"

Roark said he did know that, but Stan talked right over him. "Actually, novels exaggerate that a lot. In real life, you don't always smell it."

"But this isn't real life, that's the whole point!" Stasia snapped at him. "This is almond flavoring. As I'm sure you know, Stan."

She turned back to Roark. "We use it sometimes, you know, for the game. The rule is, if your victim notices the smell, they don't eat or drink whatever you've put it in, and then they don't get poisoned, and you get caught. But if they only notice it once they taste it, they do get poisoned, and they die. Which just means they're out of the game! It doesn't mean you really kill them!"

Stasia broke down again, and it took several minutes for Roark to calm her before she could go on. "So we look for creative ways to slip it to them, you know, obviously. Today I ordered vanilla-almond tea. I knew I had a really good chance of fooling her anyway, because even though our characters were rivals, Violet wouldn't have suspected me of coming after her on the second day we were here. Usually if we're going to do something drastic, we build to that. And preferably give people a chance to play for as long as they can."

"And did she smell it?" Roark asked. "The flavoring?"

"No!" For a second, Stasia's voice sounded almost triumphant over her win. Then her chest hitched with another sob. "It's tricky, you know, because you have to use a lot, so the other person can't deny that it was in there, and they know you've gotten them. So it has to be strong enough to taste, but not strong enough to smell. So it's tricky." She cleared her throat. "I already said that, didn't I? That it's tricky."

"That's all right, ma'am," said Roark. "Take your time."

"Today was perfect," Stasia said, "because we were outdoors, and you know, you never smell things as easily outdoors as you do in an enclosed space. And the teapot was covered, so I'm sure that helped."

"So you put the flavoring in the teapot?" Roark asked.

"Yes. I slipped it in there when she went inside to go to the ladies' room. And then when she came out, I pretended to drink it first, so she wouldn't suspect anything. It was just us sharing the pot, we were the only two at the table."

"But you never actually drank the tea, at any point?"

Stasia shook her head. "No. And Violet didn't suspect, until she drank it. *Then* she knew."

"And how did she react?" Roark asked.

"I'd been so afraid she would be mad. It really was kind of low of me, to try to knock her out of the game so soon. But Vi ..." Stasia grabbed a tissue from the pocket pack Roark had set on the table and blew her nose. "Vi was a good sport. A perfect sport. She laughed and said ... she said ... *Look at you, clever girl*!"

As she broke down into another sobbing fit, I saw Percy in the hallway outside the ballroom's propped-open doors, with Plant in tow. Feeling Plant's wiggles and wags might be inappropriate to the occasion, I hurried out to intercept them.

"You should probably take him back upstairs," I whispered, when I'd finished greeting both of them. "I'm guessing he won't be welcome at a crime scene."

"But this isn't the crime scene," Percy pointed out, then shrugged. "I just thought you'd like to have him with you."

He wasn't wrong about that; my dog had doubled as my security blanket since he was a puppy. And not to make Violet Kilkelly's murder about me, but I *was* still a tiny bit freaked out by the sight of a corpse. I reached down to scratch Plant's head. "Having him with me certainly doesn't hurt. Thank you."

He gave me a quick flash of his dimples. "Welcome. So what's going on in there?"

"One of the guests is confessing to fake-poisoning Violet, as her character, with almond flavoring that was meant to be fake cyanide. But she says she didn't real-poison her."

"Do you believe her?" Percy asked. "I heard the crying as I was walking up, and it sounded a little, I don't know ... extra."

I lowered my voice, even though we'd already been talking way too quietly to be overheard. "I'm not sure what I think. It's a pretty big coincidence, if somebody else real-poisoned Violet with real poison at the exact same time Stasia was fake-poisoning her with fake poison."

Percy pointed at me. "Unless they knew she was going to do it, and thought the almond flavoring would mask the smell or taste of the poison."

"Yeah, I thought of that too, but ..." I trailed off, not sure how to finish that sentence. I'd meant it when I said I didn't know what to think. I didn't know Stasia.

I didn't know any of them. Including Violet.

"... bottle in your possession the entire time?" Roark was saying as Percy, Plant, and I slipped into the room. Roark was wearing a pair of gloves now, and a plastic evidence bag sat on the table, presumably containing the almond flavoring.

Percy gave Gwen an awkward nod and a half smile as we joined them by the wall, but didn't say anything. She gave him a half smile back—dueling Baird dimples.

"Yes," said Stasia. "Well, not at dinner last night, I suppose, but it was locked in my room then. And it was brand new. Look."

She pulled a small, crumpled paper bag out of her purse and shook it out. A box and a slip of paper fell onto the table. "I still had it in the bag I bought it in. You can see I just opened the box, and that's the receipt, you can check the date. I bought it yesterday, on my way into town. I'd been planning this for a while."

While Roark gathered up the box and the receipt, Stasia closed her eyes tightly, as if she could make it all go away. "I thought I was so smart." She took a long, shuddering breath. "But you'll note I'm freely admitting to putting this flavoring in the tea, which I obviously would not do if I'd just killed my best friend. And let me say again, it was a *new bottle*. So it couldn't have been this that ... did that to Violet."

"*Nothing* did it to her," Maryjo insisted, from the table where the other guests sat. "It was an aneurysm. You'll see. A brain aneurysm."

"Enough already with the aneurysm, you imbecile!" Mitch snapped. "That is not what an aneurysm looks like."

Maryjo raised her chin at him. "How do you know what an aneurysm looks like? Have you ever seen one?"

"Mitch is right," said Stan. "It wasn't an aneurysm, it was murder. She had convulsions. And her face was a weird pink. That's cyanide."

Maryjo's attempt at a brave face abruptly collapsed, and she started to cry. Plant padded over to her and licked her knee, and she leaned down to bury her face in his neck. I didn't blame her; I knew from experience that Plant had fizzing comforting skills. He'd taken a liking to Maryjo, I mused, right from her arrival. Maybe that meant she wasn't the murderer. Or maybe it just meant she smelled like bacon.

Stan shifted his gaze to Roark. "Which means she was poisoned while she was at the gazebo, because cyanide is fast. You only need to test what she ate and drank at tea. And if it was in any shared food, she might not even have been the intended victim. You'll need to look into all of that. All depends on what carried the poison—"

"Respectfully, sir," Roark interrupted, sounding more annoyed than respectful, "the cause of death hasn't been established yet. And it won't be established by you." He turned back to Stasia. "We appreciate your honesty in coming forward with the flavoring."

Goldie, who'd been silent since we came indoors, burst into hysterical laughter. She didn't stop for maybe a solid minute, while everybody else, even Roark, just stared at her.

Finally she wiped her eyes and said, "Honesty. You appreciate her *honesty*." Another bubble of laughter escaped her lips, and she clapped her hand over her mouth.

But when her eyes shifted to Stasia's, her face turned to stone. "Why don't you be honest, then?"

Stasia glared at Violet's sister. Funny, I'd had the impression at check-in that they were friends. Maybe that was just supposed to be their characters. "Honest about what, exactly?"

"Oh, I don't know." Goldie tossed her hands. "How about that you've been *exactly* sleeping with your best friend's husband?"

Well, now. That was interesting.

Ray jumped up from his chair like somebody had set it on fire, spouting some curse words that I was pretty sure hadn't been invented yet in 1924.

Stasia gaped at Goldie. "What is *wrong* with you? I know you're new at this, but are you really *that* bad at telling the difference between RP and reality?"

Hm. So Stasia and Ray's characters had been having an affair. I wasn't sure how long everybody had been playing their roles; were their characters new for this story, or had they been using them for a while now?

And if it was the latter, how into method acting were they?

Ray jabbed a finger at Roark, as if poor Roark were the one who'd accused him of having an affair. "For the record, I am not a cheater."

"Sir, ma'am, everyone will get their chance to—" Roark began, but it was no good. Goldie appeared to have opened the floodgates.

"I knew it!" Mitch, apparently not to be outdone for dramatics, got out of his chair and stalked toward Stasia, his face turning beet red. "You killed her!"

Plant barked. Roark stood and held out his hands, gesturing for Mitch to back off.

Mitch ignored both of them. "She was your best friend, and you killed her! And now you're trying to make it look like some"—he waved his hands like an overexcited preacher—"zany mix-up or something, with this stupid almond story."

"Sit *down*!" Roark called. By then he was talking to more than one person. Mostly everybody was on their feet now, including one of the servers, who'd apparently been challenged (or maybe outright accused) by Stan.

They commenced shouting at, over, and around one another. Plant danced excitedly around them all, but the goofball didn't have an ounce of herding blood in him, and there wasn't much he could do.

"All of you!" Roark—whom I'd never seen be anything but mild-mannered before today—thundered. "Do not make me take out my gun!"

That got their attention. Roark pursed his lips in an excellent, probably subconscious, imitation of his boss. "Sit down. I'll be taking your statements one at a time. If you could please wait your turn."

Ray was the last to comply with this order. He glared at Goldie, chest heaving so dramatically I wondered whether he was having some sort of attack.

"That seems a little extra, too," Percy whispered in my ear.

I nodded, watching Ray. "And from what I've seen, he's a better actor than Stasia is."

Chapter Seven

It took hours for Bryd Hollow and Buchanan County's finest to process the scene, during which the garden picnickers returned with a tumult of questions I couldn't answer. I stationed myself in the entryway, next to one of the extra security guards Percy had called for, to greet them as best I could.

Frank pushed a couple of his fellow guests aside to get to me. "Where is she?" Presumably this referred to his wife. He sounded suspicious, like maybe I'd hidden her.

"They're keeping everybody in the ballroom," I said. "Or they were. I'd check there first."

Frank nodded, but made no move to go. "She's going to be a mess. An absolute mess. They were so close." He ran a hand over his balding pate. "Violet was her guardian for a few years. Did you know that?"

"No, I didn't."

"They were so close," he said again. "And now both of her parents *and* Violet are gone. Me and the kids are all she has left."

"I'm so sorry. I'm sure this will be hard on your kids, too," I said. And then, because it seemed the sort of thing people were expected to ask of parents, "How many do you have?"

"Two daughters. They both go to college, but they're home for the summer now." Frank sighed. "And yeah, it will be hard on them. I guess I'd better call them."

With that he trudged off, leaving me to attend to his fellows as best I could. While Percy dealt with security and the police and matters of logistics, I spent the afternoon trying to soothe the erstwhile role-players, now tragically (in more ways than one, in some cases) restored to their true personalities.

Thankfully, I had Plant to help me. Less thankfully, I had Stan to think he was helping me. He lectured me at length on the psychology of grief and how best to break difficult news to people. I'd like to pass on his wisdom, but alas, I retained none of it beyond three minutes after it left his mouth.

As always, I relied on food to be the balm for all hurts. With the kitchen still off limits, I prevailed upon catering (with help from the little inn's displaced dinner shift) to bring us enough to feed guests and non-guests alike; poor Roark looked like he was on the verge of collapse from dealing with the beleaguered league. Tristan and Gwen had long since been sent on their way, but Percy had stuck around. I guessed he was okay missing Gwen's triumphant (or not) return to Baird House. Or at least, he figured a murder trumped family drama.

"Perfect," Ruby said, when I checked with her about

serving dinner in the ballroom. "That'll get them all in one place again, and I want to talk to them."

I'd seen some awkward dinners in my time, but this one was a whole new level of awkward. Nobody seemed to know how to act, or whether they were supposed to talk, or whether it was okay to eat, or if they did eat, whether it was okay to appear to be enjoying it. At one point, one of them laughed at something another one said, and then clapped her hand over her mouth as if she'd just cursed in church.

There are two kinds of people, the ones who embrace food when they're upset, and the ones who shun it. Half the guests poked half-heartedly at their fried chicken and coleslaw, or just stared at it. The other half ate with enough gusto to make up for their companions. Pretty much everybody was drinking, though.

Fortified by a few bites of potato salad, Ruby went to stand at the front of the room, where on a happier occasion somebody might give a toast. Percy and I stood behind her, in case we could answer any questions or offer any help. (Plant, having proved useful that day as a sort of therapy animal, lay under one of the guest tables. I figured the ballroom wasn't technically a dining room, even if we happened to be dining in it.)

"Are you going to tell us not to leave town?" Stan asked, before he'd quite finished chewing a mouthful of chicken. "Because you can't actually do that, you know, to people you haven't charged. Whatever you may have seen on TV."

Ruby didn't even bother to hide the roll of her eyes. "I assure you, Mr. Bolozky, I did not rise to the position of Chief of Police with nothing but a television education in police work. I—"

"He's got a point, though," Mitch cut in. "The LARP is obviously over. We're just ourselves now, sitting here." His voice broke a little. "Without Violet, because she's dead."

As if anybody needed that reminder. I noticed Ray jerk in his seat, like he'd just been bitten by something. But he didn't say anything.

"This is really the main reason I wanted to speak with you all," Ruby said. "So it would probably go faster if you let me speak. Legally, none of you are prohibited from coming or going as you see fit. You can check out any time you like."

"But you can never leave!" Clarice practically shouted, then dissolved into laughter. She was a mousy woman whom I'd heard speak maybe twice since she'd arrived, but either the wine or the shock of the day's events, or both, seemed to have loosened her up.

"What is she talking about?" I whispered to Percy.

"It's a lyric from an old song, I think."

Whatever the joke was meant to be, nobody else got it. Clarice shrank back in her seat, turning red. I signaled one of the servers, and suggested they might want to slow down the rate at which they were refilling glasses.

"... if you could stay the week, since you were planning on doing that anyway," Ruby was saying.

"But that was when it was a vacation," said Maryjo. "Mitch is right. For once. It doesn't feel right to stay in this beautiful place without Violet."

"I understand, and I'm sorry for your loss," Ruby

said. "But staying is the best way you can help us get to the bottom of what happened to your friend. Having access to all of you would help us a lot. Even if you can just stay through tomorrow, that would be a big help. We'd like each of you to come by the police station to be interviewed, separately."

"Again?" Goldie asked. "And what about Violet's funeral? You expect us to just hang around here, rather than transport her home and make arrangements?"

"We won't be able to release the body for a few days, regardless," said Ruby.

"What about those of us who weren't at tea?" Frank wanted to know. "You want to talk to us, too?"

Ruby nodded. "We want to talk to everyone."

"And do we need lawyers for this"—Mitch made finger quotes in the air—"talk?"

"I can't tell you not to bring an attorney," said Ruby. "But if you want my personal, unofficial opinion, I'd say it'd be a waste of your money. I know the police presence here may have given you a certain impression, but at this stage we do not officially have a homicide, and our interest in each of you is only as a witness. We want to get a good sense of the Gatsby League in general, and Violet in particular. Everybody's individual impressions would be helpful."

"Our *impressions*?" Ray wailed. "My *impression* is that my wife is dead, and that you're relying on, what, gossip from these people to find her killer? That's the sort of justice I can expect from this two-bit town?"

Mitch stood, looming over the table in what I'd come to recognize as his usual manner, looking like he was going to punch Ray. (Again.) "You have some nerve demanding justice, when it was *your girlfriend* that killed Violet."

"That's a disgusting lie!" Stasia cried. She raised her chin. "A pair of them, actually. I'm nobody's girlfriend, and I did not poison Violet. Not for real, anyway."

"Maybe it was your boyfriend, then," Goldie muttered.

"Ladies and gentlemen, if you please!" Ruby snapped. "I realize this is a difficult situation for everyone. I am heartily sorry for that. But the best way to help us get justice for Violet is for you all to remain calm and leave the detective work to the professionals."

She looked Mitch square in the eye. "I hope it goes without saying that we will not tolerate violence of any kind, as I'm sure Mr. Baird and Ms. Biggs here will agree."

Percy and I both indicated that we did, in fact, agree.

"To that end," Ruby went on, "and out of an abundance of caution as well as to ease your minds, I've arranged for an officer to be here at the inn at all times."

"We've called in extra security, as well," Percy added.

"Meaning ... you want us to keep staying *here*?" Clarice asked. "I thought you just meant Tybryd. You want us to stay in this house?" She waved a hand. "Hotel, hall. Whatever."

"Oh, come on," said Stan. "It would obviously be more sensitive to move us to the hotel proper, if you're going to ask us to hang around." He pursed his lips at me. "Any amateur should realize that."

"I wish we could," I said, ignoring the jibe. "But it's

Memorial Day weekend. We haven't got rooms for all of you. Or even a fraction of you. The hotel is booked solid."

"So we're just supposed to rely on your so-called extra security?" Stan set his jaw and tipped his chin at Percy. "You need more and better cameras than what you've got. Entrances and stairwells isn't enough."

I wondered if it still counted as mansplaining, if it was to another man. Stansplaining, I guessed.

"I'll take that under advisement," Percy said smoothly.

"Are you at least planning to feed us properly, if we stay?" Mitch tossed a chicken bone back onto his plate, by way of punctuating his point. Which I guessed was that fried chicken wasn't good enough for him, even though the fried chicken was in fact very, very good.

"The kitchen will be available to use for breakfast," Ruby said. "We'll have finished with it by then, and since the incident didn't occur in the building, there's no reason you can't use it more-or-less normally. The gazebo and the area by the pond will stay taped off for now."

"As if we'd ever want to see the gazebo again, anyway," said Goldie. She crossed her arms and leaned back in her chair, as if considering Ruby's proposal. "But I for one wouldn't mind having us all kept here, together, until we find the truth of what happened to my sister. And no one else should mind it either, unless they have something to hide."

Mitch snorted. "Or unless they think they might be next."

"Don't be ridiculous," said Maryjo, who was still

insisting Violet must have died of some tragic natural cause. She tilted her head to one side. "But you know, I have a thought."

"I doubt that," Mitch shot back.

Maryjo narrowed her eyes at him. "I just *thought*, if we're going to stay, and stay together, let's do it for a reason. If Violet's body can't be released right away, she won't be able to have a funeral right away, at home, like she should. So let's have her first funeral here. A memorial dinner."

She looked at me, brows raised. "Maybe Thursday? That was supposed to be our last night here, and it would give you some time to plan it."

"I think that's a great—" I started, but was interrupted by Stan before I could get the word *idea* out.

"I am not planning that far ahead. This whole situation is way too volatile for that." He tossed down his napkin and stood. "I'll give you a day or two, Detective." ("Chief," Ruby corrected, but he ignored her.) "But for now, I'm going to bed. I'm sure I don't have to point out that it's been a long day."

The others dispersed shortly afterward, nearly all with promises to stay at least until they spoke to the police again. Of the six guests who'd been at tea, all but Stan agreed to remain until their original check-out time of Friday morning.

Ray went a step further, and declared his intention to stay "as long as it takes." He followed this vow with a lengthy apology to Ruby for his behavior. Which struck me as odd, because once you accounted for the circumstances, he hadn't really behaved that badly. I was sure Ruby had heard worse.

While he did that, Goldie came to me to make an apology of her own. Her eyes were red, the skin beneath them dark. She looked like she'd aged ten years since that morning. "I'm sorry. I know I'm probably not helping any more than Ray is. I'll do my best to let you all do your jobs."

"Don't worry about us," I began, but she cut me off with a bitter laugh.

"Oh, I'm not the least bit worried about you. No offense. But your police chief is right: the best way to cooperate is to be, you know, cooperative. For Violet's sake." Her lips trembled a little as she added in a whisper, "I can't believe this is happening."

"I'm so sorry," I said. "Frank told me you and Violet were very close."

She nodded. "I was still a minor when our father was killed, so Violet had to become my official guardian until I turned eighteen. It was just the two of us."

"I'm so sorry," I said again, because I had no idea what else to say.

A shudder ran through Goldie's body, as if she'd given herself a little shake. "Where's Frank?" She looked vaguely around. "We're going to go up, too. We want to talk to our girls again before bed."

As we watched her and Frank depart, Percy leaned down to press his lips to my ear. But he wasn't being romantic. "Did Goldie just say their father was 'killed?'" he murmured.

I nodded. "I spotted that, too."

"So like, killed-in-a-freak-train-accident killed, or murdered killed?"

"That would be the question," I said. "Because it's kind of a weird coincidence if two members of the family were murdered in separate crimes, wouldn't you say?"

Chapter Eight

It wasn't that I was grieving Violet Kilkelly, exactly. I hadn't even known her. But seeing her body had left me shaken, and I had to release that tension somehow. Some people might have chosen yoga or a treadmill or something, but I preferred a good old-fashioned crying jag. Which was what I had, the second I finally closed my door behind me that night.

Percy hadn't even wanted me to stay at the little inn, but I'd been firm on that point. I saw no risk in it, for me or for anybody else. Violet's murder was obviously personal. It wasn't like some crazed flapper-hating serial killer had joined the Carolinas Gatsby League with the express purpose of poisoning *everybody's* tea.

Besides, I could hardly assure the guests it was safe for them to stay there, then flee the first chance I got, could I? I thought Percy would see that, but he seemed perfectly willing to make himself and his resort—to say nothing of his security guys and the Bryd Hollow police force—look bad, if it got me to come away with him.

In the end, I accused him of using the murder as an excuse, just so he wouldn't have to face the drama of Gwen's return on his own. I thought it was a pretty good joke, but he didn't seem as amused by it as I was.

And anyway, I had Plant to defend me. And to comfort me; he was not up to the task of handing me tissues, at least not at the rate that I required them, but he had other skills. Namely, head-butting me to express his concern and, when that didn't have whatever the desired effect was, chewing on my toes.

All the crying left me with a headache of titanic proportions. I barely had the energy to take Plant out to pee, but pee dogs must. It was midnight by then, maybe later, and I didn't see anybody except the security guard I passed on the stairs, and the cop who was in the front sitting room, near the entrance.

Despite my protestations of safety, I couldn't say I loved being outside alone in the dark. I kept imagining somebody jumping out from behind the bushes to accost me with twenties slang and a bottle of poison. Or maybe a yellow car would come barreling up the drive and run me down, Daisy Buchanan style.

After that I just lay in bed, Plant on (*on*, not *at*, as was Plant's way) my feet, and tried to picture anything other than Violet's staring eyes. Which meant I pictured almost nothing else. Maybe it was a false impression, what with her eyes being wide open in death, and the convulsions that had preceded that death, but she'd looked so *surprised*. Not even afraid. Just surprised.

All in all, I was at somewhat less than my very best the following morning. Especially since I got up at five, to make sure I was in the dining room before anybody else. I wasn't great on four hours of sleep, as a rule. It turned out I was even less great on four hours of sleep after a murder had been committed on my watch.

I stuck to my no-dogs-in-the-restaurant policy, and arrived alone. The breakfast shift and I set the tables back in their usual formation of two-tops and four-tops, and removed as much of the twenties paraphernalia as we could reasonably carry. Some of the larger stuff would have to wait, but even so, by the time we were finished it looked more or less like a real, regular restaurant. We put regular menus on the tables, too, as a sign that the planned schedule of events had been dispensed with.

The guests started to trickle in, most of them with shoulders hunched, or arms folded over their chests, looking uncomfortable and embarrassed. They were still wearing twenties clothes, having brought little else, and the costumes felt a little grotesque under the circumstances.

I greeted them in the soft tones of a funeral director, hoping that was the respectful way to act. Honestly, I had no idea how I was supposed to behave. Not that it mattered; none of this was about me, obviously, and nobody paid me much mind.

Ray was the first to arrive. There were no wild displays of grief or outrage this time; he was silent and subdued, meeting neither my eye nor, as far as I could tell, anybody else's. He had coffee and dry toast, then went back to his room.

He was long gone before Goldie and Frank came down, which was probably for the best. They didn't say much, either. I inquired after their daughters; they said they were fine, and awaiting details on the funeral, which of course Goldie had no information about yet. She seemed offended that Ray, and not her, would be making the arrangements.

Pretty much everybody was as quiet and awkward as I was, apart from Stan, who spent a good twenty minutes stansplaining both my job and Ruby's. He was the first to leave for the police station, which was fantastic for me and almost certainly awful for Ruby. What a way to start the day.

It was Sunday, and the Bairds normally went to church as a family, so I was surprised when Percy came into the restaurant, unshaven and dressed in jeans and a t-shirt. I didn't kiss or even hug him in front of the grieving Gatsby League, but it took no small amount of restraint on my part.

"What are you doing here?" I asked him.

"Attending to Tybryd's guests in the midst of their crisis, like a good Baird should. You didn't call me last night."

"I didn't."

"Did you cry?"

"I did."

He stuffed his hands into his front pockets. "You should have called me, then."

"Why, what would you have done?"

"Pointed at you and laughed."

"I'll try to remember next time."

He gave me a subtle smile, the dimples only half lit, before going to greet Goldie and Frank, then Maryjo, then Stasia (sitting alone, drinking coffee and not eating). He made his way around to everybody, offering his condolences and asking if there was anything more Tybryd could do to help them through this difficult time. Luckily for him, Stan was gone, so it didn't take as long as it might have.

His duty done, Percy came back to join me by the wall, where I was just sort of ... standing. He seemed more comfortable in difficult situations than I was, so I took it as a good sign when he leaned back against the wall and crossed his arms. Clearly standing around was the right thing to be doing.

Goldie did a few rounds of her own, after she finished her breakfast. She came over to us last. "I was wondering, did you find the comb?"

For a second I just blinked at her; I'd forgotten all about Violet's missing hair comb. "No. I assumed that was part of the game, and whoever had taken it would return it."

"Well, they didn't. And nobody's admitting to being the one who took it, either. I've been asking around."

"I'm sure it slipped their minds," Percy said. "Yesterday was a difficult day for everybody."

Goldie scowled at him. "Yes, I'm aware that it was a difficult day. I do not need to be told how difficult a day it was."

Percy's face instantly took on his very-serious-hotel-billionaire look, which aged him and made him look more like his father than I generally preferred. "Of course. I'm sorry."

"Oh, it's fine." Goldie flashed a smile, small and tight,

but it looked genuine. "I never know what to say to people either. It's maddening, isn't it?"

"We'll do a search for the comb," I promised—fully expecting that search to be in vain. If one of the players had taken it, it was most likely in their room, and I couldn't just be searching guests' rooms willy-nilly. Stan had been right about that much. "If it's in any of the common areas, we'll find it."

"I'd appreciate whatever you can do," said Goldie. "I guess I can report it to that Ruby woman, if it doesn't turn up. It was a family heirloom, you know, passed down with some jewelry. I've told Violet a thousand times over the years that I don't want her role-playing with it, but ..."

She drew in a soft, breathy gasp, and her face fell. Like she'd just remembered, again, that Violet was dead. "And now look. She's not even here to take her rightful *I told you so.*"

APART FROM THEIR visits to Ruby, I wondered what the guests were going to do all day. On the one hand, they couldn't exactly have fun without looking cold and callous. On the other, they were on vacation, so fun was pretty much the only thing they had to do.

I, on the other hand, had plenty of work. Including pulling together a memorial dinner by Thursday. And finding the Kilkelly sisters' precious heirloom.

They say you should always look for a thing in the last place you saw it, so while I took Plant for a quick bathroom break, Percy went to talk to the supervisor of the cleaning crew, to see if they'd found anything in the game room whence the comb had, apparently, vanished into the ethereal plane.

As it turned out, not only had they not found anything, they hadn't set foot in there at all since the LARP's first (and only) night. They hadn't gotten to it before yesterday's tea, and after tea it wasn't exactly a priority. Especially with all the overtime required to give the kitchen a thorough cleaning after the police finished with it; the guests had required reassurance that no poison could have accidentally made its way into their breakfasts.

The police had been in the game room, but I had the sense their searches of the irrelevant rooms had been on the fast and possibly perfunctory side. And anyway, they hadn't been looking for a hair comb. To their eyes, it would have been just another twenties prop to be ignored.

Percy and I agreed that there was no finer Sunday activity than sifting through the detritus of a Gatsby party in hopes of finding something that was very unlikely to be there. Plant was even more enthusiastic for this mission than we were pretending to be; he trotted ahead, woofing softly as he charged into the game room.

I frowned. The room was empty. "That's weird. It was like he was greeting somebody."

"Maybe there's a ghost," said Percy.

Maybe there was. There was nobody else in here, and no other exit besides the door we'd just come through. I looked around, eyes narrowed.

Then nodded at the window. One of the floor-length burgundy drapes was tied back with a gold tassel. The other was loose, pulled partway across the window. I walked over and yanked it back.

There was nothing behind it except glass.

"That was quite a little flourish you did there, when you pulled it." Percy was clearly trying (although maybe not very hard) to quash a laugh. "What did you think, you were going to reveal Violet's killer lurking in the shadows?"

"At least the comb thief, maybe."

He shrugged. "The police were in here. They probably checked the curtains over, and left that one untied."

We started moving around the room, picking things up and setting them down again, much as the aforementioned police had probably done the day before. For Plant's part, he was only ever interested in picking up things he wasn't supposed to have; there was zero fun in it if it was going to be useful. He opted to lie down in the sliver of sunlight I'd just exposed when I opened the curtain.

"So," I said. "We haven't gotten a chance to talk about your sister. How was dinner?"

Percy tilted his hand back and forth. "So-so. Could've been worse. My mom didn't immediately faint from joy, which for her is a pretty understated reaction to one of her own kids. But she said she was happy. And Elaine was really touched that it was her wedding Gwen came for. Especially considering Gwen skipped our father's funeral."

"And what about you?" I asked. "How do you feel about it?"

He tossed a cloche hat onto the table where we were gathering the guests' forgotten things, then ran a hand through his dark hair. "I feel like Gwen probably came *because* she skipped my father's funeral, and Elaine's wedding is a convenient excuse. Now that she's had some time to process everything, I think she regrets not patching things up with my mom back then."

Strictly speaking, those were thoughts, not feelings. But I decided not to press him. "Nothing wrong with mending fences."

"No, you're right. This is a good thing. My mother's never even seen her own grandchildren in person."

"But Gwen didn't bring them, right? She mentioned something to me about vacationing without her kids."

"Yeah, I guess her coming this early was partly about testing the waters." Percy smirked. "And checking for sharks. But now that she hasn't been banished in shame from Bryd Hollow, Lorenzo and the kids are coming for the wedding."

"Aw. I love a happy ending." I risked disturbing Plant and pulled back the drapes again, then shook them out for good measure. (No comb came out.) "And speaking of her coming this early, I'm sorry I wasn't able to put together a bachelorette party for Elaine. That's why they came to see me."

I considered throwing in a little comment about how surprised they'd been to hear that he and I were dating, but nobody wants to sound like an insecure girlfriend.

Not at any time, and least of all when they actually *are* an insecure girlfriend.

"I heard." Percy heaved an exaggerated sigh. "But I suppose we can let your failure go, what with there being a murder and all. And speaking of *that*"—he grinned at me—"get ready to be impressed with my detective skills."

I raised a brow at him. Sleuthing wasn't usually Percy's thing. His thing was more scolding me for sleuthing. Although *sleuthing* wasn't always the word he used.

But responsibility *was* his thing, sometimes to a fault. I'd been watching his reaction to Violet's murder: he seemed almost offended that it had happened at Tybryd. Maybe it made him feel responsible, in some way. If not for the problem itself, then for fixing it. These were his guests, after all, and their safety was his business.

"Totally ready," I said.

"Remember how weird we thought it was, that Goldie said her father was killed? So I did some searching last night."

I clapped his shoulder. "Go you! I was going to do that today. Or as soon as I got time. Which would probably mean never."

He took advantage of the proximity necessitated by the clap and kissed my temple. "Well, now you don't have to. Danny Kilkelly was murdered in 1988. And the case was—is—unsolved."

I'd leaned closer to kiss him back, but it seemed inappropriate now that we had yet another murder going on, so I stepped back again. "How did he die?"

"Bludgeoned and suffocated. But here's the weird part."

"Bludgeoned *and* suffocated isn't the weird part?"

"Not as weird as the fact that it was a kidnapping gone wrong. Not just an abduction but like a *kidnapping*-kidnapping, with a ransom note delivered to Danny's mother."

I did some quick math in my head. Violet had been born in 1968. I knew this for a fact; knew the exact date, actually, on account of an invoice I'd sent her in the amount of $326.68. *That's my birthday!* she'd emailed back. *March 26, '68. Isn't that the weirdest coincidence? It must be a good omen!*

Violet had been into omens and superstitions. And apparently not shy about her age. (Although I wouldn't have been shy about it either, if I'd been fifty-four going on twenty-five.)

"Violet would have been twenty in 1988," I said. "We know she took guardianship of Goldie, so Goldie was a minor. But regardless, Danny Kilkelly was a grown man who'd been a father for two decades. He was not a kid to be napped."

"Nope," said Percy.

"Did his mother live with them?"

"Nope."

"Then yeah, that is weird."

"I *know*!" The excitement in Percy's voice was enough to make Plant raise his head, which was not something Plant was wont to do at that hour; mid-morning was his nappingest time of day. He—Percy, not

Plant—was clearly getting into this whole detective thing. "I'm thinking some kind of mob thing."

I pointed at him. "I don't know about *the* mob, but Goldie did mention a story their father used to tell, about the family money starting with bootlegging. So I guess it's possible he was involved in some sort of organized crime."

Percy spread his arms wide. "There you go."

"What about the mom?"

"Danny's obituary mentioned he was a widower."

I put the vase I'd just flipped over (no comb inside) back on the mantel. "And I have no doubt you looked into that. Was she murdered too?"

"Cancer, like seven years earlier."

"Seven years of bad luck," I murmured.

"Huh?"

I shook my head. "Violet was superstitious. Not that that has anything to do with anything."

"Well we can't go by *relevance*, it would make my detective skills look a lot less impressive. I'm not sure any of this has anything to do with anything." Percy put his hands on his hips, head bent, the pose of either a man who was deep in thought, or a boy who'd just gotten his third strike at a little league game. "I mean, what does it actually tell us? Nothing. I doubt Violet's death was a mob hit."

I patted his shoulder. "Don't feel bad, you're new. Anyway, there's a lot of weirdness here that has nothing *obvious* to do with anything, but you know it must have something to do with everything."

"Was I supposed to follow that?"

I started ticking off on my fingers. "One, Violet was real-poisoned, probably with real cyanide, at the exact same time she was fake-poisoned with fake cyanide."

"We don't know that," Percy said. "Until we get an official report, you're really just taking Stan's word for the cyanide part."

"And Poirot's. He also knew what convulsions and pink-flushed skin meant. And as fictional characters go, Poirot is a pretty reliable source." I held up a second finger to go with the first. "Two, Violet's comb was fake stolen, but now it turns out to be really stolen." And then a third finger. "Three, Violet's father was murdered—"

"But not fake murdered."

"—and then Violet was murdered."

"Well, a lot of years apart."

"Yeah but it's weird, right?"

"Hey, I'm the one who told you it's weird. Don't go taking credit for my detecting."

"I wouldn't dream of it. My point is, just because we can't see the connections yet, it doesn't mean they're not there. You know how I feel about coincidences."

Percy scratched his head. "I seem to recall you don't think much of them."

I chewed at my thumbnail. "I suppose, technically, it's Ruby's job to sort those connections out. As in, it's not ours."

"Except it happened in my hotel."

"On my watch."

"And *you're* insisting on sleeping here, where the murderer is almost certainly also sleeping."

Now there was an argument I had no interest in reliving. I gave him a breezy smile, meant to indicate that the trivial fact of sharing a house with a murderer didn't bother me in the least.

After all, why should it? It wasn't like it was the first time.

Chapter Nine

I SUPPOSED it was possible I wasn't sharing the inn with a murderer; by dinner that night, we were down to seventeen Gatsby Leaguers, from the original twenty-one. Five more were set to leave in the morning, having had their conversation with Ruby that day.

But Goldie and Frank, Stasia, Ray, Maryjo, Mitch, and (saddest of all) Stan were all staying—everybody who was at tea with Violet was still there.

So chances were, I was indeed in a room with a murderer right that minute, as I stood at the front of the restaurant, having a quick talk with the guests while they ate. There was no reason not to; it wasn't as if they were talking to each other. Goldie and Frank were shooting glares at Stasia and Ray. Ray was resolutely not looking back at them. Stasia wasn't looking at anybody.

As usual, I felt like a complete nitwit, with no idea how to behave. It was like I'd invited people to a wedding only to surprise them with a funeral. At least I *looked* a little less like a nitwit, now that I was out of those horrible housedresses; I'd made the time that afternoon to run back to my apartment for some normal clothes (and Plant's yellow blanket, which I'd committed the dire crime of forgetting on Friday).

I cleared my throat. "So, we've been searching around for Violet's hair comb."

Nope, still a nitwit. I cleared it again. "I think most of you have talked to Goldie about it."

There was my long-lost normal-person voice. Better late than never. "Maybe somebody still has it, and doesn't realize it, or maybe it's kind of gone on too long and now you feel weird about it. But it's a family heirloom, and she'd very much like to have it back. You can give it to me, if you want to be discreet about it, or even leave it at the front desk of the main hotel, in an envelope marked for me. That way even I wouldn't know who left it."

To my not-even-a-little surprise, nobody spoke up. I set the cardboard box I'd been holding down on an empty table. "Well, in the course of searching the common rooms, we also came across a few things. I know they might seem trivial right now, but you might want them one day."

I held up a silver cigarette box. "This, for example, looks expensive."

The owner of the box, a thin scarecrow of a man named Kirk, immediately rose to claim it. Off to a good start, then. A single earring was also promptly snatched up, but nobody wanted any part of a pair of glasses that were apparently for cosmetic purposes only. Possibly their owner had left, or possibly they were simply too embarrassed to speak up—the specs looked more steampunk than Gatsby, and were hideous besides.

Next came a hat, the very same wine-colored cloche I'd seen in the game room that first night. Percy had been the one to set it with the other things earlier; I remembered him tossing it onto the table. I hadn't stopped to take a close look at it on either occasion. Certainly not as close a look as I was getting now that it was actually in my hands.

Which explained why I hadn't noticed then what I was noticing now.

Stasia got up and grabbed it, murmuring her thanks so quietly that only I could hear.

I stared at her for a few seconds, until it became obvious I was staring, at which point I moved on to a very fancy deck of cards.

But as soon as I got back to my room that night, I called Percy.

Either the volume on my phone was too loud, or his greeting was; Plant heard his voice, and immediately started licking my phone and wiggling all over the bed. I was a little breathless by the time I got him (Plant, that is, not Percy) settled down.

I told him (Percy, not Plant) about the hat, how I'd seen it the night Violet's comb was stolen, and how tonight Stasia had been the one to claim it.

"And so the courageous hat, against all odds, found its way home," Percy said solemnly. "They should do a movie. Only they should make the hat a dog."

Plant heard the word *dog* and got all excited again.

"You don't get it," I said. "Plant, down! Enough. You'll see Percy soon."

"All day tomorrow."

"What?"

"He'll see me all day tomorrow. I'll be working from the little inn every day this week. I don't want to take up the staff room, but I can use one of the parlor rooms, now that you don't need them for parties. Plant can bring a bone and nap in there with me, if he wants."

"Why?"

"Because he likes bones. And naps. Have you met Plant?"

"I meant, why would you work from here?"

"If you're there, I'm there."

"Because of the murderer?"

"Yes, Min, because of the murderer. What don't I get?"

"Oh! Right. The ribbon. You don't understand about the ribbon."

"The ribbon on the hat?"

"Yes. It was tied like an arrow."

"How do you tie a ribbon like an arrow?"

"It's like …" I started drawing a shape in the air with one hand, then shook my head. Neither of which, of course, Percy could see. "That's not the point. The point is, the way the ribbon is tied means something. Or meant something, back when these hats were a thing. It was a signal for men."

"That seems like a waste of time. Men aren't good at reading signals from women."

I snorted. "I'll let that one go. So a knot meant the

woman was married. A big floppy bow meant she was single and shopping around. And the arrow meant her heart belonged to somebody."

"So Stasia's heart belongs to somebody, is what you're saying?"

"Belongs to Ray, is what I'm saying. Maybe Goldie was telling the truth, and Ray and Stasia are lying."

"But would Stasia even know about this ribbon code?" Percy asked. "This is the same Gatsby League that was committing the very great sin of wearing polyester, right?"

"Right, and I thought the same thing. But then I thought back, and the thing is, *she* wasn't wearing polyester. She probably had the best costume of anybody that first night, even Violet. Or at least the most accurate."

"And the lack of polyester makes you think she actually knew what she was doing."

"More than the others, anyway. In which case, she might have felt safe using an old-timey signal like that, like an inside joke, maybe, or a private message for Ray. She'd have known the others wouldn't know what it meant."

Percy put on his Narrator Voice. "But little did she know, Captain History was planning her event."

I laughed. "Exactly. And there's something else. That first night, the same night she left her hat in the game room, she went to bed early. Said she had a headache."

"And that's suspicious because ...?"

"She was also mumbling something about stupid men. And that would have been right around the time that Ray and Mitch started arguing, because Ray didn't like how Mitch was hitting on his wife. Ray said Mitch touched Violet on their way into the game room, I think it was."

"Okay, so Stasia saw Ray acting jealous over Violet, got upset and hurt, and made an excuse to get away. That's our story?"

"Pretty much."

"So then that story would end with Stasia deciding to put some poison in her poison."

"Pretty much that too."

"But why would she make a point of implicating herself like that?" Percy asked. "She would know the fake poison would make her the obvious suspect. And not only did she not try to hide the almond flavoring, she actually volunteered it."

"Maybe she thought that exact question would keep her safe. Everybody would ask it, right? And then they'd say, 'Oh, she'd never do that, she must have been framed.'"

"Well," Percy said with a soft sigh. He sounded tired. I could see where a murder in his hotel and the surprise return of his long-lost-sister might do that to a guy. And his house was practically an asylum anyway, with Elaine's wedding so close. "It's *a* story, anyway."

"But you don't think it's *the* story?" I asked.

"I have no idea. I guess we'll know more when we find out what was in that bottle of flavoring."

"I guess so," I said. "But in the meanwhile, Stasia is the only person we know for a fact to have put something in Violet's food or drink. If you ask me, she isn't just the obvious suspect. I'd call her the prime one."

Chapter Ten

GIVEN the time-sensitive nature of the Violet Kilkelly case, Percy pulled some strings with the county (and the politicians he so generously supported) to expedite all the lab tests necessary to determine what had happened to her, and when. And, one hoped, by whose hand. But Violet had been murdered on a Saturday, and even Percy's superpowers did not extend to getting results from government agencies on a weekend.

Late Monday, we heard that the cause of death had, indeed, been cyanide poisoning. It would have been far more convenient if the killer had used some exotic poison that could be traced back to them, but alas; cyanide was easy to get. It would probably be midweek before results came back on Violet's teacup and water glass, Stasia's fake poison, or the myriad other places the cyanide could have come from.

In the meanwhile, I resolved to apply my own super-power. Maybe most people wouldn't have called 1988 *history*, exactly, but it was before I was born, so I decided it counted. And okay, sure, maybe Captain History was slightly less useful than Captain Rich-Guy Clout. But if my past experience was any indication, I was probably the only one around here who would look for connections between a family's past unsolved crimes and their present ones. So I might as well.

Not that I had a lot of time on my hands. For one thing, I'd made the mistake of asking about Violet's favorite foods, so I could plan the memorial menu around them. Ray, Goldie, and Maryjo all had strong—yet oddly conflicting—opinions as to what those foods were.

When at last they presented me with a list of the items they could agree on, it was the sort of high-maintenance nightmare I'd come to expect from Violet Kilkelly: king crab, buttercup squash (*not* butternut, apparently this was very important), fresh pomegranates. At that time of year, we had access to all manner of glorious fruits and vegetables, but it seemed Violet had only liked things that were out of season or difficult to get.

And then there was Elaine. With her wedding less than two weeks away now, I was receiving multiple texts a day of the *Hey, I know you've got this murder stuff going on but I just have one quick thing* variety. Gwen's arrival, and the imminent arrival of her husband and two young sons, had caused ripple effects well beyond adding four guests to the list. With the boys coming, Elaine decided she'd better revisit her policy on children under ten entirely, lest some of Phil's family get offended.

Suddenly we had nearly twenty children on our hands. We needed a kids' menu. We needed a few babysitters on hand to help watch them when their parents got drunk. We needed kids' tables, which meant revising not only the seating chart, but the whole layout, really.

The wedding was to be held at Baird House, with the ceremony outside in the garden and the reception in the ballroom—which meant each of these changes needed to be communicated to Snick. He mostly answered them with two-word replies and increasingly irate emojis, until finally he sent me nothing but a hand making a very rude gesture.

The only ones who weren't demanding much of my time were my actual current, living guests. Most of them had bought a piece or two of modern clothing in town, so as to feel less conspicuous (or less morbid), and were spending their time around and about Tybryd, or hiking the trails around it. Other than Stan and, occasionally, Goldie, they didn't talk to me much.

Poor Ruby wasn't finding them quite so unobtrusive. According to my friend Paul, who got it from Roark, Ray was driving Violet's gigantic SUV into Bryd Hollow several times a day to demand justice. Usually amid a great outburst of tears.

I still hadn't decided whether I thought his overwhelming grief was genuine, or a bit too much protesting.

Despite my temporal challenges, I managed to carve out some time on Tuesday afternoon to find out what I could about Danny Kilkelly and his murder. I'd spent the morning working on wedding business in the game room, next to the window I'd been so suspicious of two days before. (Yesterday it had been the music room, but

Percy and I had swapped today, owing to his need for a quieter room in which to take a long international call. Plant was with me, rather than Percy, for that same reason.) As soon as I finished the tomato sandwich I'd grabbed for lunch, I closed Elaine's seating chart and opened my browser instead.

The Kilkelly family hailed from central New York, which you wouldn't think would be a hotbed of bootlegging activity, but I guessed between the Erie Canal and the proximity to Canada, it wasn't the very unlikeliest place to find a little organized crime. It was possible that Percy was right, and the abduction was some sort of mob hit.

It was while I was learning a wealth of information about rumrunning along the canal and across the Great Lakes that I was nearly caught by Goldie. Thankfully, Plant warned me somebody was coming. He thumped his tail twice, but didn't bother to get up from his sunny spot at my feet.

"Are you looking at something naughty?" Goldie asked as she walked in. "You slammed that laptop lid down *lickety-split*."

Odsbodikins. Here I'd been trying not to look guilty. I definitely did not want her to see me researching her home town.

"Isn't that a twenties thing?" she asked. "Lickety-split?"

"Nineteenth century, actually."

The card tables had been replaced with the room's usual, more relaxed setup, and Goldie chose the most comfortable armchair, the one I'd specifically not chosen, lest I fall asleep. She looked like she wouldn't mind a nap herself; I could've stored spare change in the bags under her eyes. "What a useless thing to know," she said, with a laugh that sounded strained.

I gave her a look of mock disapproval, hoping to encourage this bit of lightness in what had been some very dark days for her. "History is never useless."

Her face fell. "No, I guess it isn't."

I cursed myself inwardly. Of course that had probably reminded her of the Gatsby League, and Violet's own love of (pseudo)history. Why must I always say the worst possible thing, in every situation? "I'm sorry, were you looking for me?"

"No, actually, I didn't know anyone was in here. I was just coming back to the scene of the crime—the other crime, obviously—to think. This thing with the comb is really bugging me."

I hesitated to get into either crime with her, then decided she must want to talk about it. She was the one who kept bringing it up. "Do you think the theft of the comb is related to ... what happened to Violet?"

Goldie tipped her head against the back of her chair and blew out a long breath. "I've been asking myself the same thing. I don't really see how it could be. The comb is valuable, but it's not so valuable that someone would kill Violet for it. And anyway they already had it, so there would have been no need to kill her, would there?"

"No. It doesn't make much sense to me either."

"But it's weird, right?" Goldie straightened back up again. "A lot of the people who stayed back for tea that day were in here the night the comb was stolen."

"I don't think that part is so weird. The people closest to Violet were the most likely to do the same activities as her, right?"

"I'm not sure we can call them *the people closest to Violet*, considering one of them must have killed her." Goldie shrugged and looked away. "But according to the cop shows, that's not that weird, either. It's always the husband, isn't it?"

I had no answer to that. Ray was my guest, too. I couldn't go gossiping about whether or not he'd murdered somebody. Or even whether or not he'd been cheating on his wife with her best friend.

Fortunately for me, any reply I might have made was interrupted by another tail thump and a gentle *woof* from Plant, who did get up this time, to greet Maryjo coming into the room.

"Oh!" Maryjo put her hand to her chest, as if she'd just suffered a shock. "Goldie! What are you doing here?"

"Oh, you know," Goldie said in a breezy, mock-casual tone, "trying to figure out who could possibly be so callous as to refuse to return my irreplaceable family heirloom and precious memento of my recently departed sister. You?"

"Oh," Maryjo said again. She tittered, looking uncomfortable. "I see. Well. I was just looking for Mrs.—Ms.—Biggs. Minerva. Hello there, Plantagenet!"

She brightened up as Plant, who apparently felt he wasn't getting his appropriate share of her attention, started wiggling madly, his tail whacking her around the legs. Maryjo sat down in the nearest chair and bent to touch her forehead to the top of Plant's giant head, which happened to be a thing he absolutely loved. The two of them sure had hit it off.

My mouth fell open as I watched them. *The two of them had hit it off.*

Plant had gotten up for her, when he hadn't for Goldie (and wouldn't, for just anybody). Whenever we were in a room with the guests, she was always his chosen. He got excited to see her.

Excited enough, maybe, to motivate his lazy self all the way up to a trot, if he thought she was in the room he was approaching.

And he'd made that same small, soft *woof* two days ago, as he was trotting into this very room.

My eyes snapped back to Maryjo, and I was a little disconcerted to find hers were on me. Apparently she'd been talking to me.

"... some ideas for Violet's memorial. I'm glad you're here too, Goldie, because I wanted to ask what you thought, too. I thought, since a few people are still stuck with the clothes they came with anyway, maybe we could come to the dinner in character."

"I don't know that that's a great idea," I said. "A lot of your characters hated each other."

"Some of us hate each other even when we're out of character," Goldie said.

"Well then, dressed," said Maryjo. "*Dressed* in charac-ter, how about that? A final sendoff from the Gatsby League. This is *our* memorial, after all, isn't it? A special one just for us."

"A themed cosplay memorial service." Goldie

laughed. "Sounds tacky and awful to me, but Violet would have loved it. Let's do it."

"Speaking of the costumes," I said to Goldie, "you mentioned taking some pictures at dinner the first night, any chance you'll share them? Maybe I can use some for a display or a slideshow."

Goldie pulled her phone out of her back pocket and tapped the screen. "Sure, I'll send you the album."

"That would be fantastic, thank you. Also, a few of the people who've already gone home were thinking of driving back for the memorial dinner. I can email them for you guys, if you like, and let them know."

"Let them know what?" Stan sauntered into the room. Plant didn't so much as look at him. Like most of us, he didn't think much of Stan.

Stan shrugged when Maryjo told him her idea. "Whatever Goldie wants, I guess." He nodded at Goldie. "I just got back from town, figured I'd give you an update."

"I already talked to Frank, not that he had anything to say." Goldie shifted her gaze to me. "Frank's been haunting the police station every day, because Ray is haunting the police station every day, and I'll be darned if I'm going to let Ray find out something before I find out something."

"Doesn't seem to be much to find out," said Stan. "Not sure this podunk police force is up to the job, to tell you the truth." He glanced at me. "No offense."

"None taken," I said, which was a lie. I wasn't a cop, and I wasn't even a longtime Bryd Hollow resident, but I still didn't like that use of the word *podunk* to describe what had very quickly become home to me.

"There's no way they're going to have this wrapped up by Friday morning," said Stan. "You might want to consider booking another room for after that, if you want to stay on their case. We don't want them losing interest, once the victim's family isn't breathing down their necks anymore."

That was a bridge too far. "Ruby is not going to lose interest," I said. "And neither will Tybryd, I assure you."

"I already got a room anyway, at the main hotel," Goldie said with a wave.

"Oh?" I asked. "I could have made that reservation for you."

"Frank made it. Ray has one, so ..." she let that sentence go unfinished. At this point even Plant probably understood without having it spelled out for him that this game of one-upmanship was a priority for Goldie. "No word on whether or not Stasia's staying with him."

Stan snorted. "Stasia will be a guest of the county, if those police officers and their lady chief have a shred of competence between them."

So Stan was convinced that the obvious suspect was the right one. Mitch seemed to be convinced it was Stasia, too. Goldie, and presumably Frank, seemed to think it was Ray, or Ray and Stasia together.

For my part, I was still undecided on the matter. I was leaning toward Stasia, but Percy's point about her implicating herself was a good one. Hence my looking

CORDELIA ROOK

under every rock in the Kilkelly garden, hoping to shine some light on ... something.

"By the way," Goldie said to me, "your fella assured us that the room is free of charge, for as long as we need it. Either he's a classy one, or he's afraid we're going to sue him."

"He's a classy one. I don't think he's afraid of much." I tilted my head, mentally reviewing a recent experience with Percy and the great outdoors. "Snakes, a little bit."

"Giving away all my secrets for free, I see." Percy came into the room, rolling a suitcase behind him. The game room sure was popular today. And apparently everything I said carried out into the hallway. Maybe I needed to work on my indoor voice.

"You were expecting me to sell them?" I asked.

"Depends on what you were offered, I guess." Percy bent to say hello to Plant, who'd abandoned Maryjo without so much as a backward glance. Priorities.

"What's with the bag?" I asked.

"Went home to grab it after my call ended. You've got enough empty rooms now, I decided to stay out the week on site." Percy nodded at Goldie. "See if there was anything I could manage for you personally."

It sounded professional, when he put it like that, but I knew it was really because he wanted to protect me from the murderer he seemed convinced was skulking directly outside my door at night.

"Thank you," said Goldie. "At the moment, all I need to manage is finding a snack, and I can probably do that on my own."

She gave a quick wave to nobody in particular and

left. Maryjo followed, after reminding me to email the absent members of the Gatsby League about the memorial dinner. Stan stayed on to lecture Percy on the subject of gutter covers (he offered no hint as to what had brought this pressing issue to mind) before taking his leave at last.

As soon as they were gone, I closed the door and pushed Percy into the nearest chair.

His brows shot up. "Are you going to ravish me? Because I should probably grab a breath mint first. I had a meatball sub for lunch."

"You ate a meatball sub in that suit?"

"Is there a special kind of suit for eating meatballs?"

"Yes. The kind you don't have to be afraid of spilling tomato sauce on."

"You know me. I fear only snakes."

I gave him a kiss—a tame one, not of the ravishing kind—before sitting on the rug to rub Plant's belly. "There's nothing wrong with your breath, but no. Sorry. I was just excited to tell you this." I lowered my voice. "I'm thinking Maryjo stole the comb."

Percy leaned forward, elbows on his knees, looking almost as enthusiastic as if I'd just said that yes, as a matter of fact, I *was* going to ravish him. "What makes you say that?"

"It's just a hunch." I glanced around the room, ready to tell him about Plant rushing in here that day, and what I thought it meant. "Because—"

Then I stopped abruptly as my eyes fell on the door, and a memory struck me. "Wait. Maybe it's *not* just a hunch. The night the comb was stolen, Maryjo said she had a headache. She specifically said the aspirin hadn't done anything for it. Except she showed me her handbag, and there was no aspirin in it."

I pointed at the door. "They said nobody else had left the room, other than Mitch. But Maryjo must have, if she took aspirin."

"So she could have taken the comb to her room, then come back down," said Percy. "Maybe people just forgot she left, or with all the excitement between Mitch and Ray, maybe they didn't even notice."

"Exactly," I said. "And here's where the hunch comes in. The way Plant reacts to her, I think it was her that he smelled in here the other day. She could have left right before we got here. And the way the curtain was ..."

I bit my lip. "This might sound dumb, but what if she was trying to put the comb back? Like, stick it somewhere where it would be plausible that we hadn't found it already, but would still look like it was just misplaced, as a way of giving it back without admitting it was her. Maybe she was trying to see if she could tuck it into the folds of the curtain or something. But then she heard something—sound seems to carry awfully well in that hallway—or got spooked somehow, and left. She might even have been making a second attempt today. There was definitely something off about her when she came in. Especially when Goldie brought up the comb."

Percy rubbed his knuckles over his jaw, considering. "It doesn't necessarily sound dumb. Your hunches tend to be pretty good, where crimes are concerned."

I snickered. "Except that time they got you arrested for murder."

He waved this away. "Yeah, but that was just the one time. So let's say your hunch is right, and Maryjo took the comb. Does that mean she also murdered Violet?"

"On that point, my hunches are silent."

But Plant's, it seemed, were not. He thumped his tail. I looked down at him. "But I think no. Plant likes her. He wouldn't like a killer."

"But thieves are okay in his book?"

"Sure. He's a thief himself."

"True. I've lost my share of household objects and personal items to him."

"Speaking of your personal items, about that suitcase." I stood up and wiped Plant's hair off my pants. "Do you really think this is the best time to leave your house, with Gwen in town and Elaine's wedding so close?"

"Are you kidding me? It's exactly the best time. That place is a madhouse right now, and you know how Snick gets when it's like that."

I laughed. "Glad I could be a convenient excuse, then."

Percy leaned forward to grab my hand and pull me closer to his chair. "None of it's as important as keeping you safe."

I did my best not to laugh again. He was being sweet, but he was also being a little bit ridiculous. "How does sleeping one floor up, oblivious to what's going on in my room, count as protecting me?"

He gave me a small, one-dimpled smile. "Is that an invitation for a sleepover?"

"It is not." *Tristan didn't even know we were dating*, I

103

added, but only in my head. I was not in the habit of planning sleepovers with men with whom I'd had neither the *How Serious Are We* talk nor the *Where Is This Going* talk.

Not that Percy meant it, anyway. There was no greater gentleman alive; he was like a carryover from a bygone era. (Which, considering my thing for bygone eras, was probably part of his charm.)

I cleared my throat, realizing I'd let the silence go on a little long. "No offense, but I'm pretty sure Plant's a better deterrent than you are."

"No argument there. But ..." Percy shrugged one shoulder and squeezed my hand at the same time. "I told you. If you're here I'm here."

I'll allow that my heart may have melted the tiniest bit. Because I knew he didn't mean that in a stalkery, *Where you go I go* sort of way. He meant it in a *If you're in this bad situation, I'm in this bad situation* way. He meant we were a team. And he said it like it was obvious. Like it wasn't even a question.

Plant was wholly and unconditionally in my corner, always. But it felt like a long time since I'd had a human there. Had I ever? Had Percy?

I reminded myself—again—that we'd only been together a short while. And—again—that he hadn't told his family about us, other than the ones who couldn't help but notice. And that I hadn't told my family about him, either.

Although in my case, it was kind of different, because he was kind of famous, and that made it kind of weird. The Bairds were old-school American aristocracy, and

Percy was their golden boy. The man's name showed up on gossip sites from time to time. Would my family think I was bragging? Would I look like a fool if it didn't work out? (Probably not as big a fool as I would look like if it *did* work out. I wasn't exactly jet-set material.)

Not to mention, that way lay a quagmire of inquiry and analysis from which I might never escape. My sister's —and to a lesser degree, my parents'—curiosity would be at the frenzy level. I preferred to wait until we were a Serious Couple before I spread the news to people who would take it as an invitation to relentlessly quiz me about him and ask when they could meet him.

Which we weren't. At least not yet. A Serious Couple, that is.

Still. I kind of wanted to have *If you're here I'm here* stitched onto a throw pillow, or something.

Chapter Eleven

ONLINE NEWSPAPER ARCHIVES that covered the specific, somewhat obscure Finger Lakes town where the Kilkellys lived and Danny Kilkelly died were a little on the thin side. But after many searches, two paid subscriptions I would never use again, and one actual live-person phone call, I managed to find various bits of Mr. Kilkelly's story covered by Buffalo, Albany, and Syracuse papers. I put the bits together like puzzle pieces that Tuesday night, sitting on my bed and taking notes as I read.

It did not look like a mob hit to me.

It looked like something else entirely.

Like Percy had already told me, Danny Kilkelly had been bludgeoned and asphyxiated. Most likely the latter when the former didn't do the trick. They never found a murder weapon.

But first he'd been abducted, apparently from his house in the middle of the night, or late enough that his teenage daughter was asleep. Goldie was the only one living with him at the time; Violet went to college a two-hour drive away.

Also like Percy had told me, the ransom note wasn't delivered to Danny's house, but to his mother's, two streets down. Almost like it had been a child who was kidnapped, rather than a grown man. It demanded only ten thousand dollars in ransom, an absurdly low number, given Danny's considerable wealth.

There was nothing unusual about the letter's type; forensics never found anything to connect it to a specific typewriter. It instructed one member of Danny's family, no more, to go alone to an abandoned train station not far from town.

Danny's brother went. He brought the ransom, but he was never obliged to part with it. He found Danny's body around the back, alongside the overgrown tracks.

The ransom note was signed by a Mr. Johnson.

"Mr. Johnson," I said to my screen. The screen did not answer.

"Mr. *Johnson*," I said to Plant. It was after ten; Plant was way too tired to care.

I texted Percy: *Mr. Johnson!! Come to my room, you have to see this.*

The indicator that he was typing a reply showed up, disappeared, showed up three more times, then disappeared a final time.

Thirty seconds later, he was at my door, holding his head in his hands. "There were too many jokes. So many jokes. I just couldn't pick one."

I grabbed him by the elbow and pulled him inside, then closed the door behind him. "So, it wasn't a mob hit." Thankfully, Plant's greeting was subdued owing to the late hour, and I wasn't required to shout.

Percy sat at the foot of the bed. "Danny?"

"Yeah." I sat at the top, Plant wedged between us like a Victorian chaperone. "Abducted, bludgeoned, and asphyxiated, like you said. And the note went to his mother, also like you said."

"So you wanted to congratulate me on my reading comprehension?"

"The ransom demand was for ten thousand dollars."

"Okay."

"And the ransom note was signed by *Mr. Johnson*."

"And just so we're clear, I'm *not* supposed to make a joke?"

"You are not. Everything I just mentioned is a shoutout to the murder of Bobby Franks." When Percy looked blank I added, "The Leopold and Loeb case."

He shook his head. "I want to go 'Oh, right! That!' because I can see you're really excited, but I have no idea what you're talking about."

"It's a famous murder from the twenties. 1924, as a matter of fact—the same year the LARP was supposed to be set in. And not only that, but *May* of 1924. Violet died on May 28, if you need reminding."

"I don't." A line formed between Percy's brows. "1924, huh?"

"Yep. Leopold and Loeb were these two ratbags who decided they were going to prove they were smarter than everybody else by committing the perfect crime. Except they were actually pretty stupid, and one of them left his glasses like *right next* to the body."

"That is pretty stupid."

"Right? So they got caught. It's famous because of the trial. Clarence Darrow defended them, he gave this big speech about capital punishment, the judge was persuaded and gave them life in prison." I waved a hand, dismissing the politics of the case. "The point is, they beat their poor victim, who was only a boy, with a chisel and then stuffed a rag down his throat."

"Bludgeoned and asphyxiated," Percy said.

"And they sent a ransom note to the boy's parents, demanding ten thousand dollars. That note was signed *George Johnson*. And by the way, they had this whole elaborate plan, which didn't work because—"

"Because they were stupid."

"Right. And part of that plan was to have the ransom thrown off a moving train."

"That also seems stupid."

"Yeah," I said, "they were weirdly incompetent, for guys with such an unwavering belief in their own superiority. But in Danny's case, they were instructed to bring the ransom to an old train station. Almost like a little homage. So we've got this murder of a Kilkelly in 1988 with some weird echoes of a murder in 1924."

"And now we have the murder of another Kilkelly in a setting that has some echoes—a few of them weird, like polyester—of 1924." Percy scratched the back of his neck. "Did the police in Danny's case ever make the connection to Leper and Hobo?"

I kept my face as straight as I could; laughing only encouraged the man. "Not that I saw, and that doesn't surprise me. Remember, this was before the internet. I don't know how good their police databases were, but I bet it wasn't as easy as just plugging in a few search terms and finding similar crimes."

"Plus, this feels almost like a tease, doesn't it?" Percy shook his head. "That's the wrong word, but"—he started ticking off on his fingers—"the causes of death are probably commonplace, for murder victims, but probably not commonly seen together. You've got a ransom demand for the same amount, signed similarly, but they didn't actually use the name George. The ransom drop points both involved trains, but not in the same way. It's like Danny's murderer worked in just enough details for it to be clear to somebody who really knew the case, but not enough details for anybody who didn't."

"Like an inside joke." I swallowed. It was sickening, thinking about the kind of person who would find bludgeoning and suffocating a guy funny. "But Violet must have made the connection. If not at the time, then at some point since. She would have come across the Leopold and Loeb case at some point, being obsessed with the era."

"Or else that's *how* she got obsessed with it," said Percy, "trying to figure out the connection."

I pointed at him. "Maybe that's what got her killed. Maybe she dug into the wrong thing, or asked the wrong question of the wrong person." I chewed at my lip. "We need to see what we can find out about the backgrounds of the others who were at tea. Maybe one of them had some connection to the Kilkelly bootlegger. Or Erie Canal bootlegging in general."

"So we're back to the organized crime theory?"

"Could be two warring cartels, or whatever you call them. Gangs? Maybe Danny inherited some shady business from back in that day, and passed it on to Violet when he died." I shrugged. "Or maybe it's just two warring families. Wouldn't be the first time we laid a murder at the feet of a longstanding feud, would it?"

"It would not. But if it is a family thing, that would be bad news for Goldie." Percy cocked his head. "Or maybe not. She'd have like thirty-five years until the next murder."

"Somebody might want to warn her daughters, though. Maybe they only come for one Kilkelly per generation."

He drummed his fingers against his leg. "You don't think Goldie could've made the connection to Leopard and Toad, do you? She'd have said something."

"Presumably, but I doubt she knows anything about it. She's not into the twenties history. She only came to make Violet happy." I tossed my hands. "But it *is* connected, right? This can't all be a coincidence."

"Can't be," Percy agreed.

Or maybe it could. It was Tuesday night when I discovered the similarities between the murder of Danny Kilkelly in 1988, and the murder of a fourteen-year-old boy named Bobby Franks in 1924. By Wednesday morning, it was a moot point.

Percy knocked on my door before my hair was even dry, and barely kissed me hello before telling me that a contact at the lab had just called him. (Illegally, I was pretty sure, and I didn't want to know whether this was before or after they called Ruby.)

They'd found sodium cyanide in the bottle of almond flavoring.

"So Stasia …?" I left the question hanging. It didn't seem to require an answer.

But Percy answered it anyway. "My guess is, Stasia's in big trouble."

Chapter Twelve

PERCY WAS RIGHT: Stasia was definitely in big trouble. Ruby came before the guests—we were down to nine now—had even finished their breakfast that morning. She was accompanied by Roark and an arrest warrant.

The others looked on in relative silence—at least at first—while Stasia protested her innocence, and Ruby tried to get a word in to tell her her rights. Mitch was clearly delighted. Maryjo looked stricken, Frank solemn. Stan looked arrogant, like he'd personally cracked the case.

"I would never hurt Vi, you know I wouldn't," Stasia fumed, though it was unclear which *you* she was addressing. "I had nothing to do with this." She gestured vaguely toward Ruby and Roark. "I *gave* them that flavoring bottle. I *handed it* to them. Why would I have done that, if I knew there was arsenic in it?"

Percy gave me a pointed look, having asked that same question of me. I still didn't have an answer.

"Drop the innocent act," said Goldie. "You know perfectly well it was cyanide."

"Well, pardon me for being a little distracted!" Stasia snapped. "I meant to say cyanide." She gave Goldie a look that started out defiant, switched to confused, then turned aghast. "But you know that."

Roark had been doing his best to lead Stasia away, but Stasia dug her heels into the carpet, stopping short, still staring at Goldie.

"You know that because it was your idea," she said.

"What are you talking about?" Goldie stared back, looking every bit as surprised and repulsed as Stasia. "You can't imagine I had anything to do with my sister's death."

"But you did!" Stasia looked at Ruby, as if she fully expected this pronouncement to inspire her release. Instead, Ruby nodded at Roark, who gently turned Stasia around so he could cuff her. He was a nice guy, and he did it as nicely as he could, but there's only so nice you can be about a thing like that.

Stasia barely seemed to notice. "We had a whole conversation, that night we went to Scuppernong. After the last meeting. We were in that giant booth, the ..." Being unable to gesture with her hands, she swung her head in something like a circular motion. "The semicircle one. Me and you and Frank, and ... Stan, you were there."

She nodded vigorously at Stan. "And Kirk, I think? We agreed that my character would want to kill Violet's, but I said I could never pull anything like that off. Violet was too good, she'd catch me."

"Yes, I already told Chief Walker all about that

night," said Goldie. "About how *you* said you could put some almond flavoring in some tea that smelled strong, because Violet always liked those weird flavored teas, and if it smelled strong enough maybe you could work it so she wouldn't smell the flavoring."

"Of course she said that," Ray snapped. "Because that's how we always do it when we fake-poison each other."

"Not that you would know that," Maryjo said to Goldie, "being brand new here." I wasn't sure whether she was trying to make things better or worse.

"But I only said all that after *you* said I should poison her." Stasia tried to wrench herself out of Roark's grip, which went about as well as you'd expect, and ended up just sort of wriggling in Goldie's general direction. "This was you! This was all your idea."

With a snort, Goldie rolled her eyes and turned away. "Too little, too late, Stasia. You aren't going to save yourself by trying to pin this on anyone else." She tossed her head at Ray. "Not unless you want to go ahead and name your accomplice. That still won't save you, but it would be nice to watch you both fry for this."

Ray scoffed at her. "Yeah, you'd love that, wouldn't you? You only want to keep pointing a finger at me because you're hoping if I get arrested, you'll get Vi's money."

"That's ridiculous," Goldie spat.

"All right," Ruby said. She looked over her glasses at Stasia. "I think we've given you sufficient time to say your parting words. Roark."

Roark escorted Stasia away. Ruby followed, along

with the officer who'd been on duty at the little inn that morning. There was no need for the extra protection now. Somebody had been murdered, somebody had been caught. It was over.

But it wasn't, quite. Violet's body hadn't yet been released to Ray, and he intended to have her cremated locally before bringing her remains home to Charleston. It was already Wednesday; the memorial dinner was tomorrow. The remaining Gatsby Leaguers *(and then there were eight)* decided they might as well stay. In fact, five who had already gone home accepted my invitation to come back for it, and would be checking back in the following morning.

Thirteen at dinner. Violet would have hated that.

Goldie continued to treat Ray with the utmost suspicion, but everybody else's mood lightened quite a bit, all things considered. Life—and the Gatsby League—could go on now. Violet was still dead, of course, but they all seemed pretty comfortable that her killer had been caught and was being brought to justice.

Percy seemed a little less comfortable, in that regard. He'd had an early meeting in the executive building, so had missed the excitement at breakfast. But he came into the restaurant, where I was working on the layout for the memorial dinner, a couple hours later.

"Where's that boy?" he asked, looking around.

I gestured widely. "I'm in a dining room."

"Yeah, but there's nobody else in here."

"Even so. I'll have to go walk him soon, though, if you want to come."

"Sure." He scratched the back of his neck. "So I've

been thinking. We should just make sure Ruby has all the information, don't you think? We should tell her about Danny Kilkelly and Leopold and Loeb."

"Wow, no joke names? You must mean business." I sighed. "Just be prepared for Ruby not to care. She wasn't very interested in Emily Baird, remember?"

Percy stuffed his hands into his pockets and cocked his head, his face screwed up as if he were trying to catch a memory that wouldn't quite stick. "Yeah," he said finally. "I think I remember that case pretty well."

I gave him a sheepish look. Of course he did. It was his father who'd been murdered. "Right. Sorry."

"I remember that she was wrong and you were right, about the connections to the past," he said. "Suppose these connections are relevant too, and you're the only one who's seen them?"

"You don't think Stasia did it." It wasn't a question. Percy Baird was like a terrier with a bone, when he didn't want to let a thing go, and he had that terrier look about him now.

"Do you think she did it?" he asked.

"I mostly did, a couple days ago. But now, with this whole Danny-Killkelly-Leopold-and-Loeb thing?" I shook my head. "I'll say this: I think there's got to be more to Violet's murder than we're seeing."

Percy pulled his phone out of his pocket and glanced at it. "We should drop by the police station."

I nodded at the phone. "Looks like you're busy."

"I was just checking to see where we're at in relation to lunchtime. And the clock has smiled upon us; if we leave after Plant's walk, we can eat at Deirdre's after.

Did you know Tony just put truffle fries on the menu?"

"Truffle fries?" I raised my brows, intrigued. "That sounds fancy, for a diner."

"They're a spiritual experience." He put his phone away, then crossed his arms and bent his head in that way he had when he was examining something. In this case, me. "You look stressed. You could use a few hours away. And there's no harm in combining our civic duty with a little fun, is there?"

"No harm in combining it with fries, that's for sure."

Ruby Walker was—as usual—not impressed.

"Really? You really want to do this again. Uh-uh. Nope. No." She shook her head, I guessed just in case the *uh-uh*, *nope*, and *no* weren't enough to get her point across. "You are not going to make accusing me of arresting the wrong person your Bryd Hollow personality."

"I'm not saying you *necessarily* arrested the wrong person," I said. "And to be fair, the last time I told you that, you really had arrested the wrong person."

She probably didn't need the reminder, since Percy was sitting right next to me. But I could hardly be expected to resist when she walked right into it like that.

Ruby folded her hands on top of her desk. "Yes, and it was the only time in my very long and very expert career." She gave me the Glasses of Doom. "Remind me again, how long and expert has your career in law enforcement been?"

I decided answering that question was of little value. "Like I said, I'm not saying Stasia *didn't* do it. Maybe she did, maybe she didn't. All I'm saying is it seems like there's a bigger picture here that should be explored." I leaned forward in my chair. "She kept asking why she would have volunteered that almond flavoring if she'd known there was poison in it. You have to admit she has a point."

Ruby rolled her eyes. "Could anyone really be that stupid, right? That's your question? People are always asking that question—people who aren't cops."

"It seems like a reasonable question," said Percy.

She snorted. "To you, maybe, because you don't see what I see. But I am here to tell you, not only *can* people be that stupid, people *are* that stupid. They are that stupid every blessed day."

"But—" I began, but Ruby waved me off.

"That's for the lawyers to work out. I have my own job to do. The almond flavoring was brand new. Stasia herself said that it was in her possession from the time she bought it—at a grocery store not too far from here, on her drive up—to the time she opened it, which was immediately before she used it. No other almond-flavoring-related deaths have occurred anywhere else in the county." She spread her hands. "It's a pretty open and shut case, you guys."

"A little too open and shut though, don't you think?" asked Percy. "It seems too easy."

It was his turn for the over-the-top-of-the-glasses

stare. "This is not a movie," Ruby said. "We don't worry about whether it might make the third act too boring if the first person we accuse turns out to be the one who did it. In the real world, we do things like follow the evidence, and arrest people we have cause to arrest. You know, kind of like police work?"

"Exactly," I said. "You're an experienced investigator. So in your professional opinion, you don't think it's an odd coincidence that there's a twenties connection—a 1924 connection specifically—in two murders of two members of the same family?"

"Sure, I'll give you odd," Ruby said with a shrug. "But what are you suggesting?"

I knew she didn't really want an answer, but that wasn't going to stop me from giving one. "Maybe it's related to the Kilkelly family history of that period. A tie to a past crime. There was a Kilkelly bootlegger in the twenties. Maybe there still *is* a Kilkelly bootlegger. And a rival bootlegger."

Ruby pursed her lips. "I know you like to live in the past, but surely you've noticed that Prohibition is over."

"Or it could be a family thing," I said. "Revenge for some old grudge."

"Which could be a problem for Goldie," Percy added. "Especially if you've got the wrong person in jail right now."

Ruby shook her head. "Nothing in the story you just told me suggests I have the wrong person in jail. Maybe you're right, and the murder of the father is connected somehow to the murder of the daughter. That might be some interesting motive speculation to look into. But it doesn't alter the actual physical evidence, and it certainly doesn't override it."

Now I tried a disapproving look on her (to no effect whatsoever). "Stasia would have been what, fifteenish when Danny Kilkelly was killed?"

Percy looked at me. "Who in the Gatsby League *was* an adult when Danny was killed? Maryjo, I would guess. And Stan."

I grinned at him. "Oh, I would love if Stan did it."

"Can you imagine?" Percy flashed his dimples at Ruby, who had possibly suffered at Stan's hands more than any of us. "Can *you* imagine?"

Ruby's lips might have twitched the tiniest bit. "Don't you threaten me with a good time." She looked back at me. "But you know as well as I do, there are a thousand ways the cases could be related without the same perpetrator being involved. The last time you brought me a past murder with a connection to a present one, the original killer had been dead for a hundred years."

I was actually going to agree with her on that, but she held up her hand to stop me before I could even get the first word out. "Look, I'll tell the DA about this Leopold and Loeb thing. If nothing else, he'll find it interesting. I imagine Goldie would find it interesting, too. Feel free to share."

Ruby pressed her palms against her desk and stood, which I knew from experience meant we were dismissed. "Thank you both for coming in. A pleasure, as always."

I couldn't help but feel that last bit wasn't entirely true.

Chapter Thirteen

"SHE THINKS WE'RE NITWITS," I said.

Percy and I were walking down Honor Avenue toward Deirdre's, leaning so close together we were lucky we didn't trip one another, his head bent down toward mine as we talked. It was the only way we could be heard above the oldies the town streamed through the speakers at the base of each tree, without shouting loud enough for all of Bryd Hollow to hear.

"She's always thought we were nitwits," Percy said. "So no loss there. But the bottle of flavoring—" He cut himself off. "Hey, Allegra! Aaron!"

I looked up to see a young, golden-haired couple a split second before I would have walked into the stroller the man was pushing.

"Per*cy*!" the woman—Allegra, apparently—squealed. She wrapped him in a tight hug.

Percy pecked her cheek, then stepped back and put his arm around me, pulling me close to his side. "Do you guys know Minerva?"

I briefly analyzed this presentation. He hadn't used the word *girlfriend*, but he'd left no doubt that we were together. Did he not want to give me a label? Was he afraid I didn't want a label? What did it mean, in the context of the Tristan thing?

"No, we haven't met!" Allegra gave me a warm smile.

"Allegra and Aaron Callender," Percy provided as I shook hands. "We went to high school together." Of course they did. Everybody in Bryd Hollow went to high school with everybody.

"Are you new to town?" Allegra asked me.

"As of last fall. I worked at Noah's Bark for a while, and now I'm at Tybryd." I left off that I'd started out working for the Bairds. I knew there'd been a lot of gossip about me, when I first came (and got Percy arrested). If by some chance these two didn't know about me already, I wasn't about to be the one to tell them.

"That explains why we haven't met," Allegra said with a laugh. "We've barely left the house since then."

Aaron gave Percy a solemn look. "I'm so sorry we didn't make it to your father's funeral. And for your loss, of course."

"Thank you," said Percy. "I think you get a get-out-of-funerals-free card when you just had a baby what, a week before?" He crouched in front of the stroller, where a baby girl sat, hunched to one side, clutching a bright orange teething ring in one plump hand. She already had a mop of honey-colored ringlets that many a grown woman would have envied. "So this is Hannah."

"Yep," Aaron said, then added with obvious pride,

"She's in the ninetieth percentile for height! She's going to be a tall one."

Percy smirked at him. "Wonder where she gets that." Aaron was well over six feet tall. Like, basketball-player over.

"And I'm pretty sure I haven't sent you a thank-you note for the baby gift yet," Allegra said with a grimace. "Eight months later. I'm sorry."

Percy stood and waved this away. "Don't be silly, I get it. I mean, I can't *get it* get it, having never been in the situation, but I've heard enough stories to get it. You are hereby excused from sending me a note."

Apparently disapproving of this lapse in manners with regards to her gift, Hannah started to fuss. Percy and I both tried to distract her with funny faces, but apparently neither of us was any good at it, and she started to cry in earnest.

Allegra gestured at her husband. "Give it to me, I'll just give it to her now."

Aaron reached into a plastic shopping bag slung over his wrist and handed her a box of liquid ibuprofen. Glancing up at the shops behind them, I realized they must have just come out of the drug store.

While Allegra worked her way through several layers of safety seals to get to the medicine inside, Aaron turned back to us. "It's not you, it's her. She's got a little fever today, it's made her cranky as all get-out."

"Oh, yikes," Percy said. "We won't keep you, then."

We parted ways with mutual assurances as to the niceness of seeing and/or meeting one another. I waited until we got a few steps up the sidewalk from them, then looped my arm through Percy's and tugged him toward me. "The flavoring."

He leaned his head back down, in conspirator mode once again. "What about it?"

"You tell me. You were saying something about it, before we ran into them."

"We don't have to talk about how cute the baby is first?"

"I don't know, do we?"

"I don't know, women always want to talk about how cute the baby is."

"That's very sexist of you. But she is very very cute."

"All right, box checked. So the flavoring. Ruby's not wrong when she says nothing can contradict physical evidence. How do we explain cyanide getting into a brand new, closed bottle, if Stasia didn't put it in there?"

"We can't," I said. "But it's not *impossible*. She didn't have the bottle on her every single second, right? Somebody could have snuck into her room and tampered with it."

"Maybe. I guess." Percy opened the door to the diner and stepped back to let me go through first. "We'd have gotten them on a security camera though, right? Ruby and Roark already checked all the footage from Friday and Saturday."

"I—" I stopped to smile at Tony, the barrel-chested, hairy-armed man who ran Deirdre's. "Hey! Haven't seen you in a while."

He walked right past me to clap Percy's shoulder and shake his hand. I took no offense. Where Bryd Hollow star power was concerned, I could never hold a candle to

Percy. The town was practically feudal when it came to its founding family.

His homage to his Baird overlord duly paid, Tony nodded at me. "Twig. You guys want a booth?"

"That'd be great," I said.

"And I can tell you right now that we'll start with truffle fries," Percy added. He took my hand, twining his fingers through mine, as we made our way to the booth Tony had jerked his chin at.

Which reminded me. (Again.)

I slid into my side of the booth and cleared my throat. "You never seem to have a problem with Bryd Hollow people knowing we're ..." I waved my hand, unsure what to call it out loud. "... knowing about us."

Percy's brow furrowed. "Why would I have a problem?"

"I don't know." I looked over at the tabletop juke-box, inspecting it like I'd never seen one before. "Seemed like it might be a secret."

"You all need menus?" Tony set two waters down on the table. He had two other servers working the lunch shift, but he always waited on Percy himself.

Awkward moment for an interruption, Tony. Percy and I both declined the menu and ordered (FGBLT for me, cheeseburger for him), then affirmed that we did indeed want the sides of fries that came with the meals, despite having already ordered truffle fries to share.

Tony went off to see to it. I sat there like the bumbling nitwit I was, avoiding Percy's eye.

Percy reached across the table to take my hand. "Why would it be a secret?"

I shrugged. "Tristan didn't know."

He looked confused again. "Tristan was in St. Thomas for like the whole month of April. I didn't tell you that?"

"No." *And now I feel super stupid.* "Nice for him."

One side of Percy's mouth quirked up, setting off the dimple. "Trust fund babies, am I right? Anyway I hadn't talked to him in ages when he showed up. And you know Tristan. Taking an interest in people other than himself isn't really his thing. I guess it just never came up."

"About the security camera thing, though." It wasn't exactly the most elegant transition, but I was in something of a hurry to change the subject. As I might have mentioned, *insecure girlfriend* wasn't my favorite look.

Percy narrowed his eyes, as if considering whether to let this go. The decision went in my favor. "What about it?"

The thing with the security cameras was this: the little inn only had four floors, and had been built with a more intimate, bed-and-breakfast-style atmosphere in mind. Unlike the main hotel, which had security cameras everywhere, the little inn only had a handful. One at the entrance, and the rest in the stairwells and the lone elevator.

All of the stairwells, in fact, but one. "That front, mansion-looking staircase that goes from the first floor to the second doesn't have a camera," I said. "And Stasia's room was on the second fl—wait a second."

I'd said that last bit because I'd just remembered something, but the second of waiting turned out to be mandatory anyway. Our drinks arrived just then, along

127

with the truffle fries. The latter were piping hot, and had a heap of freshly grated parmesan on top.

As soon as Tony was out of earshot again, I said, "So get this, Stasia was originally supposed to be on the fourth floor. But she didn't want to be that close to Violet, so Maryjo volunteered to switch with her."

"Okay, but try these, though."

I tried one. Which led to three more. Percy had not been wrong about the truffle fries.

While I engaged in a display of slightly questionable table manners, Percy leaned back and took a long sip of his unsweet tea. "So you're thinking Maryjo swapped on purpose, so she could get to Stasia's room without being caught on camera?"

I bit my lip. "I don't know, when you put it like that. Maryjo doesn't seem quite that ..."

"Manipulative?" Percy provided. "Clever?"

I shrugged, feeling bad for saying it. "But appearances can be deceiving. If she really stole the comb, she might be some kind of criminal mastermind disguising herself as a sweet harmless lady."

"She'd have to be a criminal mastermind, to get into Stasia's room, even if she did get up there unnoticed. She didn't keep a key to the second-floor room, did she?"

"No, I had everything in envelopes, and I definitely saw them switch. I don't know, maybe we're overcomplicating this. Probably Stasia really did do it." I drummed my fingers against the table. "But that doesn't mean we know why. If it was just to get Violet out of the way to clear the path to Ray—and I can't say Ray seems like a good enough catch to commit murder for—then this whole business with Danny Kilkelly's murder wouldn't be connected at all."

"And you're not buying that," said Percy.

"I'm really not." Although I couldn't have said why, other than my usual insistence that the past was living among us at all times. It wasn't a terribly specific connection; the only thing the two murders had in common was a passing reference to 1924. And not even the same reference.

But something about it was nagging at me.

And if that wasn't reason enough, it was also nagging at Percy, who was way more sensible than I was about that sort of thing. "I'm not buying it either," he said. "But let's say we're right. Ruby's not investigating anymore. Nobody but us is paying any attention now. And our suspects are all leaving on Friday morning, right?"

"Right."

"Well." Percy gestured with the fry in his hand, accidentally flinging a gob of dipping sauce onto my phone, which was sitting on the table. "You know what that means, don't you?"

"I do. It means we have ..." I tapped my phone (smearing the sauce) to look at the clock. "Oh, forty-three—forty-five at the outside—hours to solve this crime."

BY THE TIME we got back to the little inn after a long lunch that included not only fries, and then fries again with sandwiches on the side, but also banana pudding, somebody from the station we'd just left a couple of hours before had beat us there. A police car was parked in front of the entrance.

And an ambulance.

I frowned. "What's going on? Why didn't somebody call me, if something was wrong?" I pulled out my phone. "Odsbodikins, I missed two calls. I must have put it on silent by accident when I was cleaning your sauce off my phone."

"I got sauce on your phone?"

I didn't answer; I'd already picked up my pace. What if there'd been some sort of wide-scale kerfuffle, and the ambulance wasn't the whole picture? "I hope Plant's okay."

"Plant is fine," Percy assured me. "They wouldn't call a person ambulance for Plant."

"Plant is a person!"

"*I* know that, but ..." He left the sentence unfinished and turned his attention instead to a Tybryd security guard at the door. "Al, what happened?"

Al looked from Percy to me and back again. "They told us not to let anyone else in or out, but you guys are probably okay, right?"

"Probably," I said, then repeated Percy's question. "What happened?"

"I heard one of the guests had a stroke, but now they're saying it was—" Al stopped abruptly to move out of the way of two paramedics coming out the front entrance, wheeling a gurney.

My stomach did a little flip. Was what? Another poisoning? Something else?

Not an aneurysm, I bet.

I saw the patient as the paramedics sped past us: it was Maryjo. She was unconscious. They had her hooked up to what looked like a portable ventilator.

My stomach churned again. I had the fleeting, disconnected thought that the banana pudding might have been a mistake. Maryjo's neck looked bruised.

I went to grab Percy's arm, but he'd already grabbed my hand.

He bent down to whisper in my ear. "It's an ambulance. It's not the medical examiner's van. She's breathing." He squeezed my hand tighter. "She might need help to do it, but she's breathing."

I nodded—my own breath seemed caught in my throat, and I couldn't answer him.

Apparently, fate did not consider being required to solve a murder in the span of forty-three (forty-five at best) hours to be a sufficient challenge for two very amateur and largely unqualified sleuths.

It had decided to give us some sort of assault to solve, for good measure.

Chapter Fourteen

Maryjo had been strangled. By somebody who didn't know much about strangling people.

Not that I knew much about strangling people either, at the time. But I learned a few things that afternoon, mostly from Roark and a little bit from the internet.

Here's the thing about strangling: it's harder than it looks on TV. Strangling takes hand strength. And strangling takes *commitment*.

You've got to keep up the proper amount of pressure not for seconds, but for minutes, before your victim dies. And they'll pass out well before that, so if you don't know what you're doing, and aren't very good at taking a pulse, you might think they're dead when they are, in fact, not.

Maryjo wasn't dead, but it seemed possible she was on her way. She'd been deprived of oxygen for long enough that there would be brain damage, the severity and permanence of which remained to be seen. If she regained consciousness at all, she might or might not be able to identify her attacker.

Possibly motivated by a desire to get us out of her hair, Ruby asked me and Percy to take Roark to pull the security camera footage, which was a bit of an undertaking. The security office was its own standalone building, utilitarian and nondescript, way on the other side of the grounds beyond the winery. We brought Plant with us (mainly to get him out of the inn, too) and led the way in Percy's old Jeep, while Roark followed in his car.

We didn't talk much on the way. The banana pudding was still sitting very uneasily in my stomach.

The supervisor on duty set Roark up in front of the biggest monitor in a room full of big monitors. Nobody told Percy and me we had to leave—how could they, really, when he owned the building—so we stood behind Roark's chair, watching over his shoulder while Maryjo took the elevator up to the fourth floor. Judging by the time stamp, she would have just finished her lunch.

She never came back down.

The only other people who'd been on the fourth floor between when she'd gone up and when she'd been found were those whose rooms were also there: Ray, Mitch, Goldie, and Frank.

One of them had attacked Maryjo. The real carri-witchet was why. Percy and I had just been talking about the possibility of Maryjo sneaking into Stasia's room and tampering with the flavoring. What if she'd killed Violet, and somebody had found out and decided to kill her instead of turning her in?

It was one possibility among many. Maybe she'd

found out something dangerous. Maybe she'd discovered either the real killer, or Stasia's accomplice. Or Ray could have done it, just to give the impression there was still a killer on the loose, and clear Stasia's name.

"Who found her?" I asked Roark.

He tugged at his ear and mumbled something about not being sure he should share details of an investigation with us.

"But we're not suspects," I pointed out. "We were at Deirdre's, as Tony will tell you. And it's not like we're just curious bystanders, either. Don't you think it would be a good idea to give us as much information as you can, for ...?" I looked at Percy and waved my hand in a turning motion. *Keep this rolling for me, will you?*

"Security," he provided. "I'll obviously need to change up the monitoring, and the shifts at the inn again. They'll want me to tell them as much as I can. Right, Hal?"

He gave the security supervisor a pointed look. Hal agreed that information always made his job easier.

Roark rolled his eyes at the three of us, but allowed that he couldn't actually see any harm in telling us a few things, either. "Mitch found her. She was slumped outside the door of her room, like she'd collapsed on her way in. Medics thought it might be a stroke or some such, until they saw her neck."

"And nobody heard anything?" I asked.

Roark shrugged. "Not that they'll admit to."

"Hmph." I chewed at my thumbnail. Maryjo was a pretty small woman. Somebody could have strangled her elsewhere, and then dumped her outside her room.

Mitch could even have done it, then "found" her to draw suspicion away from himself.

Although, he'd seen how confessing to any association with the crime had worked for Stasia. Still. He seemed like the strangling type.

Whoever had done it must have known there were no cameras in the hallways. Either that, or they weren't bright enough to think of cameras, which given their ineptitude at strangling was a possibility.

All of which I pointed out to Percy when we were alone in the Jeep again. Although I might have been hard to hear over how obnoxiously loud Plant was panting. Apparently his investigative efforts had exhausted him.

"On the bright side," I said, "I guess we should be glad we don't have a seasoned pro on the loose. That does kind of put a wrench in our mob theory, though. Whoever attacked Maryjo was definitely not a hitman."

Percy drummed his fingers against the steering wheel. "But everybody probably knows there're no cameras in the hallways. Stan stansplained it at dinner, the day Violet was killed."

"Oh, right." How could I have forgotten? "And I'm sure he's brought it up with everybody more than once since."

"He's brought it up with me more than once since, I can tell you that. And he's not even wrong, but with Memorial Day and the short work week, Hal hasn't been able to get more cameras installed yet."

"Bit of a closing-the-barn-door-after-the-horse-got-out situation anyway, isn't it?"

Percy snorted as he pulled into the inn's parking lot.

"Apparently not. Apparently assaults at the little inn are going to be a regular thing now."

I tipped my head back against the seat and closed my eyes. I really didn't want to get out of the car and go back in there. "It does make you wonder about the murder of Danny Kilkelly though, doesn't it?"

"In what way?" Percy asked.

"Whoever killed him clearly thought *they* were a seasoned pro. So good, in fact, that they could take Leopold and Loeb's so-called perfect crime, and succeed where those two donkeys failed. Top the uber-men, and all that."

"A crime of arrogance."

"Exactly." I squeezed his arm. "Nice turn of phrase. And what could a crime of arrogance have to do with a botched strangulation? Nothing, probably, that's what. I'm probably just reaching with this Leopold and Loeb obsession."

"Maybe. But on the other hand, Stasia can't have attacked Maryjo from jail. Which means we were right about at least one thing." Percy unbuckled his seatbelt and turned toward me. "This case is nowhere near as open and shut as Ruby thought it was."

ONCE AGAIN, the guests found themselves in the middle of an active investigation.

Not to mention finding themselves under a roof where two of their number had been attacked, and one of those killed.

We gathered them together in the largest parlor this time; we hardly needed the ballroom now, with so few of us. Plant made his rounds around the room, sniffing at everybody, then threw himself at my feet with a heavy sigh. I realized, with a little twist in my gut, that he was probably missing Maryjo.

I expected them to laugh in Ruby's face, if she asked them to stay at the little inn. (An expectation Ruby apparently shared, because she did not ask.) I expected them to get in their cars the very instant they were dismissed. Most of them lived in Charleston, a five, maybe six hour drive, depending on traffic. Even as the afternoon wore on, they could've been home in time to sleep—presumably safely—in their own beds.

At the very least, I expected them to accept our offer of another place to stay. Things were a little less crowded at Tybryd mid-week, and we could have gotten them rooms in the main hotel. Or if they preferred, gotten them rooms at an entirely different property. Nobody would have blamed them.

But to my very great surprise, and probably Ruby's too, and definitely Percy's, five of the remaining seven *(and then there were seven)* declined to do any of those things. Ray, Mitch, Goldie, Frank, and Stan declared that they would not budge from the inn. The two others took rooms at the main hotel, but otherwise intended to finish their stay.

Not only that, but they were determined to go forward with tomorrow's dinner.

"We can't *cancel*." Ray looked scandalized by the very idea. "Whatever the circumstances. It's Violet's memorial. The league was like family to her. This dinner would have meant a lot to her."

"It meant a lot to *Maryjo*." Stan, who frequently mocked and belittled Maryjo, who only a few days ago had practically thrown a tantrum over the request that he stay, now crossed his arms and gave me his most belligerent look. "And you don't know. The brain is an amazing organ. It heals. She could *be here* for it. Imagine if she came back, after all that, and found out it was off." He shook his head. "Uh-uh. No way. We're not canceling it *now*. Not for anyone, not for anything."

Nor were they the only ones who felt that way. I got a text from a married couple who'd gone home on Monday, and already declined to come back for the dinner. The news about Maryjo, which had apparently spread like wildfire through the league, had changed their minds, and they wanted to be sure the invitation still stood. I assured them that it did. Two extra meals was no big deal, and if they wanted to stay until Friday morning, heaven knew I had the rooms.

When you considered that three of the original twenty-one guests were now either dead, hospitalized, or in jail, fifteen coming together for dinner was quite a rally.

Everybody's affection for Maryjo seemed to have gone up three sizes that day. Much like with Violet, they didn't want to leave town without making sure some justice would be done. And unlike with Violet, there was now a certain defiance about them, of the *If we allow ourselves to be driven away, the terrorists win* variety.

Well. Most of them felt that way—and one of them was faking it.

Maybe that had something to do with their determination to stay, too. Maybe once one person said they were staying "for MJ," the others were afraid they'd look guilty if they said otherwise.

When the police left, leaving behind a number of questions they either couldn't or wouldn't answer, those questions fell on me and Percy. Pretty much all at once.

"Are they going to drop the charges against Stasia now?" was the first thing Ray wanted to know.

"Why would they?" Mitch asked.

Ray tossed his hands. "I don't think her arms are long enough to choke Maryjo from the county jail!"

"You don't know that Maryjo's attacker and Violet's murderer were the same person," Mitch countered.

Stan scoffed. "So, what, we just happened to have two attempted or actual murders in one week, among a group of close friends?"

"Speak for yourself on that 'close friends' thing." Goldie was talking to Stan, but as usual, she was glaring at Ray. "Of course what happened to Maryjo is related to what happened to Violet, but that doesn't mean Stasia is innocent. If she wasn't working alone, for example, her accomplice could have gone after Maryjo. Maybe he even did it specifically to throw suspicion off his lover."

I had to keep myself from nodding; I'd had a similar thought earlier. But as their host, it felt like my duty to remain neutral and objective.

Ray had spent most of the week either weeping or staring blankly into the middle distance. Sure, he'd gotten angry here and there, but I'd seen no sign of the brash role-play character who'd punched Mitch that first night.

But apparently he'd reached his limit, because that man came out in full force now. He leapt at Goldie with a speed that shocked us all.

Including Frank, who tried too late to get between them and ended up being pushed onto the floor for his trouble. Plant barked at them, but stopped shy of the fray, play-bowing as if hoping this was a game.

Thankfully, Ray didn't physically attack his sister-in-law. But he did get right up in her face to shout several obscenities, peppered with proclamations that he couldn't stand her anymore, that she was a liar, that he would never have hurt Violet, never, ever, and nor would Stasia. That they'd been loyal, they'd done everything Violet ever asked of them, they'd sacrificed everything for her.

That last bit was interesting. What had they sacrificed for her? And how much did they resent it?

"You don't know the first thing about sacrifice, or about family," Goldie snapped back. Not one to be intimidated, she stepped closer to Ray rather than back from him, and started doing some shouting of her own.

Percy put his hand on Ray's shoulder, easing him backward. But Goldie only advanced, closing the space between them again. Frank's pleas that she stop making a scene went unanswered.

"Goldie." I took one of her arms. Gently, as Percy had been gentle. All we wanted was to nip this before it escalated into something security had to get involved in.

But then Goldie and Ray jerked away from us, both at once. Before I knew it, I somehow (owing to my own lack of grace, no doubt) ended up between them. Ray's elbow smacked into my temple. I reeled back with a cry.

Percy was having none of this. To say nothing of Plant.

Apparently unsure which of my opponents he was meant to attack, Plant jumped between Ray and Goldie, no longer barking (which, if they'd known him, they'd have known was actually a bad sign), but snarling with no small degree of menace.

"Plant, *hold*," I snapped.

He settled on Goldie, possibly because Percy already had Ray in what seemed to be some sort of wrestling hold. Plant got down on his haunches in front of her, giving her another warning snarl, looking very much like he might leap up at any moment and rip her throat out. Goldie went white, and absolutely still.

I instructed Plant to stay, and assured Percy that I was fine.

"But I've had enough," I added, looking from Goldie to Ray. "Believe me, I understand that these are trying circumstances. I feel for you both, I really do. We're all doing our best here. But we simply cannot tolerate any violence. If you don't think you can comply with that, I'll reiterate our offer of other accommodations."

Goldie lifted her chin. "We didn't actually get *violent*."

I snorted, which was probably unprofessional, but I was pretty much beyond caring. "Tell that to the lump on my face. Don't worry if you can't spot it, it'll be purple in a minute."

"Minerva," Ray said, with the utmost dignity despite the fact that he was standing in an extremely awkward position, with his head firmly in the crook of Percy's elbow, "I am deeply sorry I lost my temper. It has been, like you said, a very trying few days. I'd like to stay for Violet's memorial, if I may, and I assure you that nothing like this will happen again."

I raised my brows at Goldie.

She tossed her head. "I can ignore him, if he can ignore me. I have faith that he won't get away with this."

"Oh, I have faith, too," Ray said. "The truth—Will you let me go, please?" Percy (grudgingly, by the look of it) released him, and Ray straightened with a grimace, stretching his neck from side to side. "As I was saying. The truth will come out. I can wait for it."

Could he, though? Because from where I stood, it sure looked like time was running out. And the truth might just run with it.

Chapter Fifteen

I stood outside Frank and Goldie's room, to which they'd retreated after Goldie's fight with Ray. My knock was tentative; I was nervous. I didn't know how Goldie would react to me poking around her family history. And I certainly didn't want to agitate her more, which the suggestion that her sister's murder might be related to her father's was bound to do. Heaven knew we'd all had enough stress for one day.

On the other hand, I didn't want to wait any longer. The afternoon's events had kept me from researching the other Gatsby Leaguers' backgrounds, but here was one thread I was pretty sure shouldn't be dropped. What if the Kilkelly family was being targeted? Ruby didn't seem to think Goldie was in danger, but I couldn't be sure. And anyway, shouldn't Goldie be given the opportunity to assess that for herself?

Goldie answered the door, red-faced and puffy-eyed. "I'm so sorry to disturb you," I said. "But would you have a minute to speak privately?"

She stepped back and waved me inside. "As long as 'privately' doesn't mean without Frank, sure."

I bit my lip. I had meant without Frank, actually. But it didn't matter; I could see the bed beyond the small seating area at the front of the room, and Frank was on it, apparently napping. Maybe she'd just meant that she didn't want to wake him up to kick him out.

Goldie gestured toward one of the chairs before taking the other. "Is this about the investigation?"

"Sort of, but probably not in the way you think." I cleared my throat. "Let me start by apologizing for bringing up an upsetting topic, at a time when you've already got more than enough to deal with. But I wanted to talk to you about your father. About his death."

Goldie's eyes shot wide. "Why?"

"Well. I came across some details about his case—"

"Came across them how?"

Yeah, this was going to be every bit as awkward as I'd feared. "Well, you had mentioned that he was murdered—"

"Pretty sure she never used the word *murdered*," Frank called from the bed. I turned in my chair to look at him. His eyes were still closed, but my razor-sharp powers of perception told me he wasn't sleeptalking. I guessed it still didn't matter. Even if I'd seen Goldie alone, she was bound to tell her husband about the conversation anyway.

"Maybe you said *killed*," I conceded.

"So you what, searched the internet?" Goldie huffed. "Thought you'd indulge a little morbid curiosity?"

I tugged at the end of my hair. "I wouldn't put it that way."

"How would you put it?"

I could feel my face heating, and I knew my cheeks must be turning as red as her eyes. But there was really no point in trying to sugarcoat it. "How I'd put it isn't important. It would still come down to me being a snoop. But I wouldn't be here admitting to snooping if I didn't think I had something important to tell you."

She waved one hand with a flourish, as if to say *Have at it, then*.

I told her about the similarities between her father's murder and the Leopold and Loeb case, stressing that those similarities were clearly intentional. "It's just, I wasn't sure if anybody had made the connection back then," I finished. "And you told me you're not into all this twenties stuff, so I wasn't sure if you would know."

Goldie still looked irritated, but now she looked baffled on top of it. "And you thought I needed something in my back pocket for the next trivia night I went to, or what?"

"Seriously." Frank got up and came to stand behind his wife's chair. "Why would you come in here and make a point of dredging all this up, now of all times?"

"I just thought you should know," I said. "With both murders being connected to this specific period in history, it seemed like somebody could be ... well, I've ..." I coughed into my fist. "There was a murder here in Bryd Hollow last year, that had a number of similarities to a past murder. And that turned out to be because the murderer was trying to make a point, so—"

"So you thought somebody poisoned my sister to make a *point*?" Goldie made a disgusted noise.

Frank glared at me. "What is *wrong* with you?"

I stood. Obviously I'd overstayed my welcome, which wasn't all that welcoming to begin with. "Look, it's up to you whether you want to draw any conclusions, and what conclusions those might be. But I thought, if there's even the smallest possibility that your family is being targeted—that *you* could be targeted—that I should tell you."

Goldie blinked at me. "Oh." She looked back at Frank. *"Oh."*

Apparently, the fact that she was the last Kilkelly breathing hadn't stood out to her until I mentioned it.

FRANK AND GOLDIE announced their intention to go into Bryd Hollow for a late dinner, saying they needed a night off from Tybryd. Mitch and Stan decided to join them. Ray left, too, although he didn't mention where he was going.

While I'd been literally scaring Goldie away, Percy had been down at the security office, making a new plan for the little inn: two guards per floor, starting immediately, with permission to pull them from other parts of the estate if nobody wanted some overtime. Ruby was sending her own detail back, as well. I doubted there was a safer place to be found in Bryd Hollow that night.

As it turned out, Percy didn't feel quite the same way. When our respective tasks had been seen to, he found me in the darkening ballroom, sitting on the floor in front of the wall of floor-to-ceiling windows with Plant stretched out in front of me.

"What are you doing in here?" he asked.

I nodded at the mountains rising in the distance. "I like the view."

He sat down beside me and leaned forward to rub Plant's belly. "I was expected for dinner with the family, but it'll probably be leftovers by now. You want to come back with me?"

I shook my head. "I'm not hungry."

He put his arm around my shoulders and gave me a squeeze. "We had a big lunch."

"That we did. But you'll text me right away if you hear anything about Maryjo, right?"

"I doubt I'll hear anything. Or that any of us will. It's private medical info, at this point." He let go of me and scratched the back of his neck. "Not that it matters."

I turned to gape at him. *"Not that it matters?"*

"Obviously it *matters*, that's not what I meant."

"Okay, what did you mean?"

"I meant there's really nothing else you need to know *tonight*."

"Ah." I stood and stepped up to the window, leaning my forehead against the cool glass. I knew where this was going, and I really didn't have the energy for it.

"You already know the only fact you need to," Percy said. "Which is that somebody dangerous is still here."

"Give it a rest, will you?" That came out a little harsher than I'd intended, but I was tired. "I can't leave. You know I can't. Not if they aren't."

"No."

"No you won't give it a rest?"

"No you can't stay here. I won't allow you to."

"Allow m—did you just say *allow*?" I turned around to find him standing, arms crossed, giving me maybe the most combative look I'd ever seen on his usually sweet face.

I crossed my arms right back. "You did not just use the word *allow* in relation to me."

Plant, sensing some bad vibes between his favorite people, sat up with an anxious whine.

"Sure I did. Why not? It's my building." That combativeness looked an awful lot like straight-up arrogance now. Throwing around his clout like the king of the castle. It was a little too reminiscent of his father for my liking.

I scoffed at him. "Maybe so, but I am not your person!"

His face immediately fell. He looked a little bit like I'd slapped him, actually. Which confused me, until I remembered the colloquial use of "your person."

Odsbodikins. "Percy," I started, but he cut me off.

"It's fine, don't worry about it." He shook his head, his jaw working. "You know what, do what you want. If you want to stay here—"

"I *have* to stay here," I corrected, but he ignored me.

"—and put yourself at risk, go nuts."

I tossed my arms. "You're seriously mad at me because I'm doing my job?"

"No, I'm mad at you because I love you."

Everything seemed to jump up several inches—my

stomach was where my heart should be, and my heart was in my throat. "I ... you ..." I swallowed my heart back into its proper place, and crossed my arms again. "Well, you've never mentioned it."

He waved one hand. "Well, now you know."

"Well, I love you too."

"Well ... great."

For a second we just stared at each other. Then, in mutual recognition that we'd somehow managed to create the least romantic moment ever, we both burst out laughing.

Chapter Sixteen

You'd think that would've been the end of my fight with Percy. But you'd be wrong.

It *seemed* like we'd made up, what with the I-love-yous and the subsequent canoodling. So we both just sort of assumed we had. He assumed I would do what he wanted, and be fine with it. I assumed I would do what I wanted, and he would be fine with it.

It was a lot of assumptions. None of them played out.

We did not part on great terms. He must have gone home for his leftovers and stayed there, because he wasn't in his room the next morning. I didn't see him at the inn.

But I did see his sisters. I was on my way out bright and early, without even having stopped to eat breakfast, when I ran into Elaine and Gwen at the front entrance.

My heart sank a little. If Elaine was coming to see me in person, it could only mean she wanted a change (or more likely, an addition) to her wedding plan that was too big to explain over the phone or text. And at just over a week from the event, we were definitely too far along for changes of that size.

Especially when I didn't really have any mental space to spare, what with all the murders and assaults and nitwit boyfriends I had to contend with.

"Min!" Elaine said. "You're just who we came to see." As if I might have otherwise thought she'd come to visit one of the guests. She nodded at the purse on my shoulder. "Going somewhere?"

I nodded. "Pen To Paper. Deb did a framed poster of Violet for me, for tonight's memorial. I need to set it up before the florist comes this afternoon, he's going to do a whole thing around it."

"Perfect!" said Gwen, which confused me. Did she have strong opinions about flower-and-poster arrangements, that she found me in compliance with? She elbowed Elaine. "Pen To Paper would be a good stop for us."

"Oh! True." Elaine gave me that wide, gummy smile she seemed to think was the key to getting her way. "How big is this poster?"

"Um. Big?" I squinted as I tried to remember. It was the sort of thing I should have known off the top of my head, especially considering I'd already paid for the thing. But I wasn't great with numbers, unless they were dates. Definitely not if they were dimensions. "Twenty-four by thirty-six, I think."

"Fabulous." Elaine wound her elbow through mine to lead me away. "That'll be way easier to fit in my car than yours. We'll all go, and then we can have breakfast at Deirdre's, so we can talk."

I definitely did not have time for breakfast. But my hands were tied, really; the french toast at Deirdre's was almost as good as the french fries. I accepted their offer and walked out with them—between them, actually, a little bit like a prisoner being escorted—to Elaine's SUV.

"So ladies," I said as I settled into the back seat and buckled my seatbelt, "don't keep me in suspense. What do you need me to get for you? Absinthe fountain? Make-your-own sloppy joe station? Creepy clown band?"

If there was one thing I'd learned in half a year as an event planner, it was that otherwise sane people would insist on doing absolutely ludicrous things with their weddings. Elaine had been relatively subdued thus far, but she had a little time yet.

"Are there creepy clown bands?" Gwen asked.

I shrugged. "I'm sure there's at least one, somewhere."

"And they can just stay wherever they are," said Elaine. "I do not like clowns. This is about Gwen's boys, actually. We thought it would be nice to give them a role in the wedding party."

My stomach lurched. There were changes that were too big for the last minute, and then there was this. "But you don't have a wedding party."

A wedding party wasn't just a few people standing at the front. A wedding party required dresses and suits, bouquets and boutonnieres. A wedding party changed the timing and flow of the event. And that whole seating chart I'd just had to redo? A wedding party would blow that right on up.

But Elaine was quick to reassure me. "No, I know. That's why we thought maybe they could hand out programs, since we can't make them groomsmen."

"They're eight and six," Gwen added. "We figured that's old enough to hand out programs without incident. Or without, you know, *big* incident."

"So you need programs." Fizzing. Maybe she'd scared me with that wedding party thing on purpose, to make this seem much more doable by comparison. Which it did. I mean, it was a lot of programs to print out. Once they'd been designed. But still. It was manageable, at least.

"See?" Gwen turned sideways in the front seat to smile back at me. "You can see how us running into you on your way to Pen To Paper is serendipity."

Was it also serendipity when we walked into the shop and found Mitch at the counter, with a bulging file folder under one arm? For me, maybe. Mitch didn't seem to consider us to be particularly well met. He scowled through my greeting, and evaded my questions about what he was doing there, and whether there was anything I could help him find in Bryd Hollow. As soon as he could politely extricate himself—or maybe a tad bit sooner than was polite—he scurried off without a backward glance.

"What was he doing?" I asked Deb.

The short, gravel-voiced proprietor of Pen To Paper shrugged. "Printing stuff off a flash drive he brought in. I didn't look at it. It was a lot of pages, though."

I frowned. "But there's a business center at Tybryd he could have used for free."

She shrugged again. "Guess he didn't want anyone at Tybryd poking their nose into his business. Seemed a little cagey with you just now."

I looked out the window at Valor Avenue, but Mitch was long gone. "Yes he did."

And why might that be?

As I often did with questions I had no answer to, I made a mental note to talk it over with Percy later. If Percy was speaking to me later, that was.

While I waited for my poster, the Baird sisters browsed through the paper and card stock on the shelves, and briefly talked to Deb about their program ideas. We continued to discuss the wedding all the way to Deirdre's, and halfway through a delectable plate of french toast.

But by the time I ordered my second cup of tea, we'd run out of things to say, and the longer and longer stretches of silence were starting to feel a little awkward. Elaine and I got along well enough, but I wouldn't have called us friends, exactly. And of course, I didn't know Gwen at all.

"So," I said as I poured a drizzle of syrup over my sausage patty, "how are things with the family?"

Elaine leaned forward, looking oddly eager. "Are you asking how Percy's taking it?"

I blinked at her. Taking what? "I ... no."

Gwen swatted her sister's shoulder. "She wants to know whether Mrs. B is super freaked out that I'm here, and whether things are tense. But she's too polite to come right out and say, 'So, is your mom super freaked out that you're here, and are things tense?'"

I stifled a laugh. As that was, in fact, exactly what I wanted to know, I decided not to bother pretending otherwise. "Pretty much."

Elaine looked disappointed. "Oh. I thought we were going to gossip about your fight."

I stiffened. "Percy told you we had a fight?"

She nodded and said through a mouthful of omelet, "He said you called him a caveman."

"I did not call him a caveman!"

"Well, he didn't use that exact word. But that was the gist of it."

I shrugged. "He was being kind of a caveman. You know how Percy can be."

Elaine rolled her eyes. "Bossy as all get-out."

"It was mildly irritating when we were friends," I said, "but it takes on a whole new dimension when it's your boyfriend. He actually used the word *allow*. Bet he didn't tell you that part."

"No, but people always leave a lot out over text," Elaine said. "Hence me wanting to get the story from you."

"Over text?" I frowned. "I thought he went home last night."

Gwen shook her head. "Nope. Skipped out on another dinner."

"Said he needed to be at the inn," Elaine added.

Odsbodikins. So he hadn't checked out, or even left the inn at all. He'd just, what? Changed rooms? And kept quiet about it, because he was afraid I'd yell at him for being overprotective.

If you're here I'm here.

I pushed a bite of french toast back and forth through the syrup on my plate. "He was worried about me, and I wouldn't leave, so ..."

Elaine laughed. "Probably slept on the floor outside your door, bless his little heart."

"Aww." Gwen pressed her hand to her chest. "I mean, don't get me wrong, I'm sure he was out of line. But—"

"But the thought of you getting hurt terrifies him," Elaine interjected.

"I think it's sweet that he wanted to look out for you," said Gwen.

"I do, too," I admitted.

"Well then, you'd better tell him so," Elaine said. "Percy needs his validation. You might recall that our father was a tad bit on the critical side."

"Oh, he was more than just critical." Gwen turned her coffee mug in her hands. "I mean, as far as Percy being protective, you have to understand. Our father ... he was ..."

Yes, he certainly was. Clifford Baird, now there was a ratbag, and no two ways about it.

"She knows," said Elaine. "She met him."

The server brought my tea, giving me a second to stall. It wasn't that I disagreed with them. I had, on more than one occasion, analyzed Percy similarly. When you grew up feeling bullied and helpless to defend the people you loved, developing a protective streak was understandable.

But should I really be getting into all of that with Percy's sisters? In my experience, he wasn't a huge fan of being analyzed. I'd done too much talking about him behind his back already.

When the server was gone again, I gave Gwen a bright look. "So, *is* your mother freaked out?"

She snickered. "Subtle change of subject."

"Subtlety isn't my strongest point."

"Well." Gwen tilted her hand back and forth. "She was a little freaked out, at first. But we've had a few good talks. I mean, a couple of shopping trips and a movie night is no substitute for family therapy, but it's a start."

"It won't be awkward at my wedding, anyway, which is the main thing," Elaine said, setting off a fresh round of wedding talk.

We finished our meal on that safe ground. As we were getting ready to leave, Roark came in and sat at the counter. He looked worn out; I wondered if he'd worked all night.

I stopped to greet him on my way past. "Hey Roark. Sorry to bug you—"

"You're not bugging me." He returned my smile, though his looked a little limp.

"Well, I don't want to interrupt your breakfast. I was just wondering if there was any more news about Maryjo that you could share?"

"There's not even any news that I can't share. I haven't heard any update on her condition at all. Ruby probably knows more." He pointed at me. "But I can share that I'll probably be by the inn later today. I want to talk to Ray about that stuff from Maryjo's purse, see if he can identify it as Violet's."

I frowned. "What stuff from Maryjo's purse?"

Roark shifted on his stool. "Shoot, I thought they'd talked to you about it. Maybe I wasn't supposed to either, then." He tugged at his ear. "Well, in for a penny. We found a bracelet in her purse that was monogrammed with Violet's initials, and there were a couple of other things with it. We think she probably took them."

"Was one of these things a jeweled hair comb?" I asked. "Or was a comb found in her room?"

Maybe my tone was too sharp, because Roark looked a little taken aback. "Nope and nope."

I made an effort to sound more casual. "Just to clarify, she was carrying this purse when she was attacked?"

"Yep. Had a light jacket with her, too, so she may have been on her way out." He paused to thank the server who set a plate of biscuits and gravy in front of him, then turned back to me. "A couple of people suggested to us earlier in the week that Maryjo might have been obsessed with Violet. Did you notice anything like that?"

"She was definitely attached to her, but I wouldn't know about anything deeper than that. She seemed— seems—like a sweet lady." *Except for that part where she's a thief, anyway.* "I'm not always the best judge of character, though. Are you guys thinking maybe she killed Violet, and somebody attacked her as retaliation?"

I'd reached the busybody boundary with that one. Roark's face shuttered. "I really couldn't speculate."

No, I supposed he couldn't speculate. But I sure could.

Chapter Seventeen

I WAS OBLIGED to bribe one of the housekeeping staff with a piece of pie I'd brought back for Percy, to tell me which room he was in. Which was kind of my own fault, because I really should have been able to guess—he was in the room right across from mine.

The rooms on the second floor were the smaller ones. The poor guy was running his gazillion-dollar empire from a full-size bed and a single chair.

And for what? So he could lie awake listening for the sound of me being strangled across the hall? What sound would that even be? I'd only seen it done in movies, and I'd just learned how inaccurate those could be on the subject, but still; I was pretty sure strangulation didn't make a whole lot of noise.

Although I supposed Plant would have—in which case, he would also have taken care of the strangler, with no need for either Percy's extra security guards, or Percy himself.

"At least then you'd have been good for something," I

said to Plant as we walked up the stairs. "You couldn't have smelled him in there last night, and told me? Or this morning? The closed door was too much for you? Do you have a cold?"

I knocked on Percy's door, still ranting at Plant. "Or are you just so used to him being around now that his scent doesn't faze you? You big dummy."

Plant took my mockery with equanimity. As soon as said knock was answered, he pranced right on into Percy's room and jumped up on the bed.

I was a little more hesitant; I stayed in the doorway. "So. Your big sisters say I'd better stop picking on their little brother, or they'll beat me up at recess."

"They say what now?" Percy ushered me in, his cheeks going pink and his expression mildly horrified. I wondered which he was more embarrassed by: his sisters, or being caught in this room.

"Well, they didn't say it exactly that way. But they were trying to help you out. I had breakfast with them this morning." I flopped down at the foot of the bed, next to Plant, then nodded at the door as Percy closed it again. "Tell me you didn't spend the whole night watching my door through the peephole."

Percy thrust his hands into his pockets. "Come on. I'll give you overbearing, but I'm not *creepy*." He became very interested in the carpet, which was a very uninteresting beige. "I wasn't trying to watch you. I was just trying to"—he shrugged, still not looking up—"watch out for you."

"A crucial preposition."

"And you know, in my defense, it's not like I was

totally out of line to worry about you. You do get shot kind of a lot."

"Twice does not qualify as *a lot*."

"You're not even thirty." He crouched down by the bed to rub Plant's ears, then looked at me from the corner of his eye. "I'm sorry for being a controlling jerk."

"I'm sorry for being stubborn and insensitive to your concerns."

"Do we get to kiss and make up now?"

We did, but I cut it somewhat shorter than I—or he —might have liked. "More kissing later. We only have a few hours until the memorial dinner, and I need to tell you something big."

Percy's eyes went wide as I told him what Roark had told me. "So you were right about Maryjo stealing the comb," he said. "She must have, if she stole that other stuff."

I pointed at him. "My thoughts exactly. She must have been our thief, she must have had the comb this whole time—so where is it now? It wasn't in her room, and it wasn't on her when she was found. But she *did* have the other stuff she took from Violet with her. So ..."

"She must have had the comb with her too, and whoever attacked her took it," he supplied, just as I hoped he would.

I spread my hands, as if he'd just agreed to my whole scheme, even though I hadn't told it to him yet. And even though he would most likely not agree to it, on account of it being unprofessional. And a slight breach of ethics. And maybe the tiniest bit illegal, although not really.

"Why just the comb, though?" Percy asked. "Why didn't they take the rest of the stolen stuff too?"

"Who knows?" I said. "Maybe we can ask them when we find out who they are. The point is, if we find the comb, we find the strangler. And we know the strangler is either Ray, Mitch, Goldie, or Frank, because they were the only ones on the fourth floor."

"But we already ruled out Frank for Violet's murder, right? He wasn't at tea with Violet that day."

I shook my head. "Doesn't matter. If we're going with the theory that the almond flavoring was tampered with, that could've been done beforehand. Somehow. In which case any of them could have done it—including Maryjo." I squinted at nothing in particular, like if I just looked hard enough, I'd find the murderer's name magically written in the air. "I still can't see Maryjo as a killer, can you?"

"Not really, but ..." Percy scratched the back of his neck. "I don't think I can make a ruling on that one until I find out who has the comb. Depends on if I can see her attacker as a killer."

"Well, her attacker is definitely a killer, considering they tried to kill her. They're just kind of a failure."

"Good point. We really need to find that comb."

I gave him a broad smile and a quick kiss. "I'm so glad you agree. It's really the only direction we can go now."

A little crease appeared between his brows. It was adorable, but not a great sign. "What am I agreeing to?"

I took a deep breath. "You've got to let me search their rooms."

"Come again?"

"Just those three!" I said, like that was somehow going to make it more acceptable. "Ray's, Mitch's, and Goldie and Frank's. One of them has it, and this is the only way to find out which one."

Percy stood. "Minerva."

"Consider that I can get access to any room I want, whether I told you about it or not."

He crossed his arms.

"But I'm choosing to talk to you about it, see, so we can agree together. Because I knew if I went behind your back you'd be mad. That has to be worth some points, right?"

"Minerva," he said again. I didn't think I'd ever told him my middle name, but I had the feeling he'd have used that too, had he known it.

I held up my hands. "There are reasons I can legally enter a guest's room without their permission. If I have reason to think illegal activity is in progress, or if they're endangering or disturbing other guests, or for maintenance."

"Yeah, I know the rules." Percy held his hand up to the side of his mouth and whispered, "My family's in the hotel business."

"I guess I don't look much like a plumber, so we can probably rule maintenance out. But that still leaves plenty of excuses. I can say I heard something. Maybe I thought an animal was trapped in there."

"An animal," he said flatly.

"Yeah, like maybe a bird flew in. Or maybe I had to test for a gas leak. There are a million things I could say.

And I'd only have to say anything at all if they caught me. Which, by the way, there would be no reason for them to do, because while they're all at dinner would be the perfect time for this."

"Minerva."

"Percy," I countered. Probably not the most solid comeback I'd ever come up with. "Come on. It's Thursday. The dinner is upon us. And then—" I spread my arms, wiggling all my fingers at the same time.

"Then they all explode?"

"No, that's *poof*." I made the gesture again. "Poof, as in poof, they're gone. And their stuff is gone with them. Which means the comb is gone. And our chance is gone."

"Minerva."

He wasn't going to let up—or give in. I tilted my head back and sighed at the ceiling. Maybe a little petulantly. *"What?"*

"You're obviously not going to search those rooms—"

"But—"

"—by yourself."

I straightened back up. "What?"

"I'm going with you."

I snapped my fingers. "Marijuana!"

Percy cocked his head at me. "I'm not sure how to interpret that."

We were in my room this time, after a few hours

spent doing my actual job and setting up for Violet's memorial. It was four-thirty. Only an hour and a half left to finalize our super secret plot to find the comb. And I had to be back downstairs for most of that.

"Marijuana is still illegal in North Carolina." I started to pace back and forth in front of my little window. "Being understandably extra vigilant right now, we were taking a walk through the inn. Doing rounds, as it were. And I happened to smell marijuana. Now not only do we have reason to believe that a guest is engaging in illegal activity, we've also got a fire hazard, which is an urgent safety issue. So we enter the room. Except"—I put my fingers to my lips and threw my eyes wide—"oops! Silly me, I got the wrong room. It must have been the one across the hall I smelled it in."

"But nobody's even in their room, in this scenario," Percy said. "They're downstairs at dinner. How could they be smoking?"

"They were smoking it earlier."

"Without setting off the fire alarm? Oh, did they tamper with it?" He looked pleased with that idea. "Because that would be illegal, too."

"Except they didn't tamper with it, because it won't have been tampered with. Unless we do the tampering ourselves, and that seems like a bad idea." I chewed at my nails, which was a disgusting habit, but this was no time to be breaking it. It helped me think. "They were smoking it near an open window. Or some of the fourth-floor rooms have balconies. I can't remember for sure about these three rooms specifically, but I think at least Ray's does."

Percy watched me with some amusement. He was usually the one who couldn't keep still. And he *was* fidgeting—mostly with Plant's ears—just not as much. "So they were smoking marijuana," he said, "hours ago, by an open window, or on a balcony ... yet the smell was still strong enough for you to catch it as you walked by their closed door."

I turned back toward him to answer, then stopped pacing. He was sitting on my bed, with Plant sprawled half across his lap. My eyes rested on the latter. "Of course not. *I* don't have super smell. Plant smelled it."

"Now Plant is a trained drug-sniffing dog? Like, an airport dog?"

"They don't know what Plant can and can't do."

"And what happens when they find out there was no marijuana in the room across the hall, either? That's worse than the smoke detector not being tampered with."

"Well, he's not a *hound*. He was mistaken." I waved Percy's nitpicking away. "This is just for plausible denia-bility. In the *unlikely* event that somebody finds us in their room. I don't think we want to waste too much time getting hung up on it."

Percy rubbed the back of his neck. "Are you sure you want to bring Plant, though? Last time you brought him into a dangerous situation, he got sent to dog jail."

My stomach churned at the memory. "That wasn't a dangerous situation. That was me being unforgivably nitwitted. And it's probably worth noting that the last time I *didn't* bring him into a dangerous situation, I got shot."

I reached down to scratch Plant's head. "Anyway this isn't a dangerous situation. Not with all the extra security guards you've got around. We'd just call for help if something went wrong. I don't think the killer can strangle all three of us at once. They are *really* bad at strangling."

"Okay, true. But that would mean we want the security guards around. If I'm not going to tell them to go on break or something, how are we going to just walk into guest rooms without them seeing?"

I shrugged. "Who says we can't let them see? You own the inn, and I'm the acting manager this week."

"Huh." Percy chewed at his lip as he considered this. "So we give them a confident wave, like we're doing something totally normal and justified and not at all wrong, and do it in plain sight." He made his *Not bad, Min* face.

I took this to mean the issue was decided. I held out my hand to him. He took it as he stood, and kissed my forehead.

And with that, we embarked on our life of crime.

Chapter Eighteen

The memorial dinner started out fine: the restaurant looked perfect, the flowers were lovely. We'd wheeled in the piano and hired a professional to play between speeches. The meal itself was five courses of Violet's very favorite things (buttercup-not-butternut squash included, an impressive feat for the third of June). Each person in attendance was going to tell a story about Violet at some point during the meal.

I'd left the tables in the smaller arrangement we had them in for regular meals; given how some of the attendees were—or weren't—getting along, one long table where everybody could sit elbow-to-elbow seemed like a bad idea. I put Goldie and Frank at the front, but on the far right side of the room, with Ray's table also in front at the far left. He was to sit alone, which made me feel kind of bad. Unless of course he'd murdered his wife, in which case he deserved it.

Mitch and Stan were the first guests to arrive in the

dining room, back in their twenties suits and looking almost subdued, for them. Percy and I greeted them in that funeral-director way we'd been practicing all week, then I played the hostess and showed them to their table. I'd put them together, closer to the back, in hopes it would discourage Stan from interrupting the speakers too much, and Mitch from threatening to punch anybody. Or from actually punching anybody. Probably a small hope, in all cases.

Frank and Goldie followed shortly afterward. Goldie, of course, made a big fuss about Ray not being there yet. "Late for his own wife's memorial? Almost like he doesn't care."

He wasn't late—the official start time was still ten minutes away—but I was nevertheless on her side on this one. The occupants of two of the three rooms we intended to search were here. I'd have liked to see the third settled in, and preferably getting a good start on dulling his senses with alcohol, as well.

In the end, Ray's arrival came last—and with enough drama to delay our room-searching plans until I could calm the guests down from the outrage several of them suffered. Namely, that he had Stasia with him.

She must have gotten bail, because unlikely as that seemed, it was more likely than Ruby dropping the charges. A daring escape after Ray sent her a cake with a file baked into it was more likely than Ruby dropping the charges.

Stasia walked in with her head high, smiling sweetly as she greeted Percy and me.

"No." Goldie marched over to us. "No, no, and no.

Get her out of here, Ray. Now." She looked only at Ray; she didn't give Stasia so much as a glance.

Ray raised his chin, sticking his lower lip out a little bit. "I won't."

"How dare you?" Goldie clenched her hands into fists, leaning toward Ray. "How *could* you? At her memorial?"

"Goldie." Frank put a hand on his wife's elbow, but she shook him off.

"She was Violet's best friend," Ray said. "She has every right to mourn her with the rest of us."

"*She* is right here, you know," Stasia said calmly.

Goldie went right on ignoring her—and fuming at Ray. I almost thought I saw steam coming out of her ears, like in a cartoon. "Petesake, Ray, why don't you just wear a sign around your neck that says *I was in on it*?" She drew an arc in the air with her palm. "*I helped my girlfriend kill my wife.*"

She and Ray looked very much like they were about to devolve into their usual shouting. Percy got between them, but in the end, it was Frank who made the peace.

"Goldie," he murmured, taking her arm more firmly now, "you need to let this go."

"Oh, *really*?" She rounded on her husband. "Why do I need to let it go, Frank? Do tell."

Frank rubbed his chin. "Well, for one thing, if he were guilty, he would act a lot more innocent, I would think. He would've been here early. And he most definitely would not have brought a date."

Goldie snorted. "I guess you have a point there."

"We are not on a date," Stasia said. "Ray was kind enough to drive me over here, that's all."

"Yeah, in my sister's car?" Goldie finally looked at her. "He bail you out with my sister's money, too?"

"Goldie!" Frank was no longer murmuring. In fact, he was downright snapping. "You're causing a scene."

"Why shouldn't I cause a scene, when they"—Goldie flung her arm at Ray and Stasia, coming dangerously close to smacking Ray—"show so little respect for my sister?"

"Because this is Violet's night!" Frank said. "If you want to talk about respect, respect that. Let's let this night be what it's intended to be: a celebration of your sister, among the people who were closest to her."

Well. And the one who killed her. I opted to keep that thought to myself.

That finally seemed to do the trick; Goldie stomped back to her table, Frank trailing behind her. Ray and Stasia sat down at Ray's table. Percy and I went on greeting everybody and seeing them settled, then waited a few extra minutes into the first course, just to be sure nobody was going to assault anybody.

Then I quietly found the restaurant manager. "I have to go and deal with something. If anybody comes to blows, will you text me?"

She agreed that she would. Percy and I went up to get Plant from my room, then took the elevator from the second floor to the fourth.

As we rode up, I tried not to stare at the red camera dot in the corner of the ceiling. "Maybe you should've just shut the cameras off," I whispered to Percy from the corner of my mouth, moving my lips as little as possible.

"There are no microphones," he stage-whispered

back, then laughed and spoke in his normal voice. "You're a terrible criminal. You look maybe the least casual I've ever seen you right now."

I deliberately relaxed my shoulders and shook out my hands.

"Anyway, we want the cameras on," Percy said. "That way if the killer catches us and kills us too, Ruby will know who was up there."

"Oh, now I'm not tense at all."

Ray had changed rooms the day Violet was killed, but he'd only moved one door down. We started there, giving the security guard we passed outside the elevator the confident wave we'd discussed. Did that look weird, I wondered, both of us waving? Probably we should plan out which one would do it, next time.

We didn't look over our shoulders as Percy swiped the keycard, or make any attempt at quiet as he closed the door behind us.

We pulled on the gloves Percy had brought from Baird House for us, even though we'd just openly walked in here, just because that seemed like a thing you would do.

I gave Plant a hearty scratch on the neck to inspire him. "All right, you, go be nosy."

He didn't seem to understand what this meant; he promptly jumped up on the bed, which was definitely going to give away that we'd been here. "Off!" I hissed. "Come on, let's look for socks."

I opened the closet and started rooting around, an activity that always got Plant interested. He trotted over and stuck his nose into each and every one of Ray's shoes. Failing to find the comb inside any of them, we moved on to Ray's clothes.

We had no luck in our section of the room. I walked over to where Percy sat on the floor, surrounded by three open suitcases that had been set against the wall, out of the way. "Violet's things?" I asked.

"Yeah."

"Anything good?"

"Nope. A lot of clothes and a couple of books. If she had a laptop or a tablet or anything, the police must have taken it."

"What books?"

"Uh … this one's about Jack the Ripper." Percy handed it up to me. "And this one looks like a biography of somebody named D. B. Cooper. Does that name ring a bell?"

I grabbed the Cooper book from his hand. "It's not a biography. Especially since nobody knows who D. B. Cooper actually was. This is true crime."

Percy stood, brows raised. "Which crime?"

"He hijacked a plane in the early seventies. He was never caught. Nobody even knows his real name or anything."

"How'd he manage that?"

"Traded the passengers for a parachute, I think, or a couple of parachutes, and some ransom money." I thumbed through the book. "Had the pilot and some other crew take off again, and jumped out as they flew."

"So he lived happily ever after?"

"Maybe." I shrugged as I flipped to the chapter about the night of the hijacking. "Maybe not. He jumped out of a plane on a stormy night, into dark woods, wearing no proper gear. There's a good chance he didn't survive the jump."

"I take it he had nothing to do with the twenties, or bootleggers, or organized crime?"

"No, and neither did Jack the Ripper, obviously. But I guess it's not surprising that Violet would get into unsolved crimes, considering what happened to her father." I knelt and started to refold a sweater he'd messed up. "Here, I'll put all this back, I'm the better folder. You go check the bathroom."

"What makes you think you're the better folder? Seems kind of sexist."

I raised my brows at him. "When's the last time you did your own laundry?"

"Never."

"Okay, then. Bathroom." I pushed Plant's face out of the nearest suitcase. "And you leave it."

I repacked the books last, and was still considering them as I zipped up the final suitcase.

"Not just unsolved crimes." I stood and pushed the case back against the wall. "Perfect crimes."

Percy poked his head out of the bathroom. "What?"

"Perfect crimes," I repeated. "Jack the Ripper. The D. B. Cooper hijacking. It's not just that they were never caught at the time. People have spent years—centuries, in Jack's case—trying to identify them, and we still don't know who they were."

"Leaflet and Blob were caught."

"But they were obsessed with the idea of the perfect

crime. And convinced they were smart enough to pull it off. Smarter than the cops, smarter than everybody."

Percy came back into the bedroom and leaned one shoulder against the wall. "Like the Zodiac. No comb in Ray's shaving kit, by the way."

"Yeah, like the Zodiac. Except ..." I turned to the window, drumming my fingers against the heater as I looked out over the garden. Ray had a very nice view. "Except like you just said, Leopold and Loeb were caught. D. B. Cooper wasn't, but he might have died, which kind of diminishes the accomplishment of getting away with it."

"So *imperfect* crimes, then."

"Or crimes that *should* have been perfect—then weren't." I took off my gloves, then pulled out my phone to text the restaurant manager. "This isn't really the time to ponder it, is it? Let's get going, the comb's not in here."

The manager confirmed that the dinner was going fine, so we decided to move on to Mitch's room without making an appearance downstairs first. We were both eager to get to it; I'd told Percy about the mysterious file Mitch had printed out at Pen To Paper.

A file that was not hard to find—it was sitting right on the bedside table. It was the first thing my eyes landed on as I closed the door behind my wagging dog.

"Who even prints stuff anymore?" Percy asked as he crossed the room. "What a waste of paper."

"I don't know, but let's have a quick look at it first, before we start looking for the comb. I'm telling you, he was being super cagey when he saw me at the shop. Even Deb noticed."

I sat at the foot of the bed, but ordered Plant to stay off. Feeling this was very unfair, Plant put his ears back and gave me a dejected look before going off to sniff everything Mitch owned. I left him to it—maybe he'd come prancing over with the comb in his mouth.

Percy sat too, both of us facing inward with the expanse of king bed between us, then spread the contents of the file across the duvet.

He whistled low.

"Odsbodikins," I said softly.

There were photographs. A few of Ray and Stasia. A couple of Goldie and Frank.

More of Violet. Many more.

Most of them looked like they were taken without her knowing about it. One was even through a window somewhere, like the pictures private detectives were always taking on TV.

Well, private detectives and stalkers.

There was also a newspaper article: one of the very same ones I'd read myself, about Danny Kilkelly's murder. I flipped it over to get to the paper underneath it. Another printout of another article.

Then printouts from three web pages about Leopold and Loeb.

I stared at Percy. "I knew Mitch was a little off, but this is kind of next level."

"Is it, though?" He cocked his head at me, as if giving this question serious consideration. "I mean, the reason you recognize all this stuff is because you've read it, too."

"But I didn't take creepy pictures! And I didn't print it all out and put it next to my pillow!"

He put his hands up, dimples flashing. "Relax, I'm just lightening up a disturbing moment."

"Ha, ha, et cetera. I guess we'll have to leave this here and call Ruby, so she can get a warrant to obtain it legally." I bit my lip. "But on what grounds will she do that? *Anonymous tip that suspect may be a weirdo*?"

"Don't know, but she'll have to figure something out." Percy gestured over all the pieces of paper—pieces of Violet Kilkelly's life. And possibly death. "But I don't think this guy is scrapbooking, do you?"

"No," I agreed. "I think this is our guy."

Even as I said it, Plant trotted toward the door with a short, sharp bark.

There was the click of a keycard releasing the lock.

I jumped up off the bed, hastily rehearsing my marijuana story (the ridiculousness of which I was only in that moment fully grasping), but I didn't have more than a split second to do it. Then Mitch was upon us, kicking the door closed behind him, demanding to know what we were doing in his room.

That part was fine. We'd planned for it.

But wouldn't you know it, the ratbag had a gun.

Chapter Nineteen

I'D SEEN a gun drawn exactly twice in my life. Both times had ended with me getting shot. So I wasn't feeling super great.

But I couldn't afford to freeze, or panic, or dwell on my fear at all. My primary concern wasn't about me or even about Percy; it was making sure Plant didn't get shot. He was growling at Mitch like this was our room and Mitch had invaded it, rather than the other way around.

I took several deep, controlled breaths. "Plant, come. Come *here*." Without taking his eyes off Mitch, Plant came to my side. "Sit. He's fine. Sit. *Sit*."

Plant clearly did not agree with my assessment of "fine," but after the third order to sit he finally did it. His hackles stayed up.

Percy moved in front of both of us. "You're not going to shoot us," he said to Mitch. "Not with all those security guards right outside."

"Well, they're not *right* outside," Mitch said. "I saw

them, they're by the elevators. But your point is taken. I notice you're not calling for help, though. Which tells me you're afraid I'd shoot at least one of you before they could get here."

True. My call-for-help plan had not accounted for guns.

Because it shouldn't have had to.

I was overwhelmed by a sudden, intense, and almost certainly irrational fury. So intense that it overcame even my fear—which, as I might have mentioned, was considerable. This was probably a bad thing, because it was the fear that was keeping my mouth shut.

But in my mind, in that moment, the outrage was entirely justified. What was Ruby Walker thinking, letting murder suspects run around with guns?

"Why do you even have a gun?" I snapped. "Why wouldn't the police have taken that?"

Mitch blinked at me. "Because I have a concealed-carry permit, and it's perfectly legal for me to have it, and they can't just go around taking people's stuff? Because no one was shot? And also they thought they had Violet's killer in jail?"

"They thought," Percy repeated, with heavy emphasis on the second word. He took a few steps toward Mitch, not looking the least bit intimidated by the gun.

Mitch glanced past him at the bed, where his Creepy Violet File was still on display. "Is *that* why you're in here?"

"So," said Percy, "how long were you stalking Violet before you killed her?"

Mitch scoffed. "You're a real pair of geniuses. I didn't kill anybody."

Percy nodded slowly. "Right. Because pulling a gun on people for being in your room is a totally normal, innocent man thing to do, and not at all because you want to shut them up about what they might have seen."

Mitch shifted the gun to his other hand, and reached into his jacket.

Odsbodikins. What, now he had two guns? What did he need two for?

But all he pulled out was a handheld recorder. "I came up here because my battery died. I have a spare in my laptop case there. I heard voices, so I drew my gun as I came in." Mitch shrugged. "That *is* a pretty normal thing to do, under these specific circumstances. You have to admit, people are getting attacked in your hotel at kind of an alarming rate."

"You're recording the memorial?" I asked. "Why?"

"Same reason I have the file. And it's not because I'm a stalker. Or a killer." Mitch pursed his lips in apparent disapproval, first at me, then at Percy. "Please. If I was going to attack someone, I'd do a better job than that. Do I look like a guy that doesn't have the stamina for strangulation?"

He didn't. He was big and beefy and ... I frowned at him. "Confrontational. Except you aren't."

"What's that?" Mitch asked.

"You're usually a ratbag."

"A what?"

"A jerk," I said. "In everybody's face all the time, picking fights."

Usually—but not right now. In fact, he looked pretty relaxed. He'd looked pretty relaxed this whole time, other than when he first came in. And other than a passing reference to us being afraid he'd shoot us, he hadn't actually threatened to shoot us.

Come to think of it, he hadn't threatened to shoot anybody. Not once this whole week. Wouldn't we already have known he had a gun, if he were really as aggressive as he'd seemed?

It was almost like Mitch had been LARPing all along, even after the LARP was over.

"Sure I pick fights. I find it's a great way to stir up drama." Mitch lowered his arm, and the gun along with it. "I don't love the idea of stirring up drama with you two, though." He slid the recorder back into his inside pocket, then nodded at the laptop case on his desk. "Go ahead and start it up. There's a file right on the desktop called *kilkelly*. Have a look at it."

Percy turned to me with a searching look and mouthed *You okay?* I gave him as confident a smile as I could. Which actually turned out to be pretty confident, now that the gun was pointed at the carpet. "You do it," he said. "I don't want to turn my back on him with you in front of him."

Plant growled—apparently he wasn't thrilled with turning his back on Mitch, either—but accompanied me over to the desk. While I booted up the laptop, Mitch went on talking to Percy. "I'm a writer."

"You're a what now?" Percy and I both asked at once.

"A writer. True crime."

"And you were looking into Violet?" I asked.

"Her father, mostly. I mean, I am part of the Gatsby League for real. But when I found out about how Danny was killed ... it's got some similarities to this old case from the twenties—"

"Leopold and Loeb," I cut in. "We know." I found the *kilkelly* file and opened it.

"It wasn't all that hard to spot," said Mitch. "Not if you're into true crime, anyway. *Mr. Johnson*?"

"I know!" I said. "And did you notice—"

Percy cleared his throat—loudly. "So you started researching Danny's case. Did Violet know?"

Mitch shook his head. "I wasn't going to tell her unless it went somewhere. But then when she was killed—"

"You thought there might be a connection," I said. "Possible bootlegging thing?"

"Eh," Mitch said, "maybe. Either way, I knew two murders in the same family was going to make for a better book."

I looked up from the paragraph of hideously purple prose I'd been skimming, and nodded at Percy. "The writer thing checks out. Sort of."

Mitch huffed at me. "Sort of?"

I gave him an apologetic look, despite not feeling super apologetic at the moment. "Your grammar's not great."

Mitch waved that away. "Who cares, that's what editors are for. I'm more like a journalist. You know. An investigator. Asking the hard-hitting questions."

"Too hard-hitting to worry about homophones, I guess. In most cases *affect* is the verb and *effect* is the noun, by the way." I bounced my index finger through the air, like I was singing along with a commercial jingle, and added, "*A* is for action."

"Thanks, I'll keep that in mind." Mitch rolled his eyes before looking back at Percy. "Let's cut to the chase. If you guys are searching rooms, I want in."

"We're not searching rooms," Percy said. "Just your room."

"Nah," Mitch said with a chuckle. "No way I was your only suspect."

Percy tried again. "Fine, you've got me. But we're done. Yours was the last one."

That didn't work either. "You didn't have time to search a bunch of rooms," Mitch said. "I wasn't even done with my second course. Give it up, you're bringing me along."

Percy snorted. "Why would we do that?"

"Well, I do have a gun."

"That there is no way you're going to use," said Percy.

"And I'm guessing you don't want me going downstairs right now and blabbing to everyone that you're doing this, do you?" Mitch gave him a smug smile. "So which rooms are we searching? And why did you want to search mine?"

I sighed, mainly because I knew the game was up. Mitch was right: we definitely didn't want the others to find out what we were up to. "Because you're on the fourth floor," I said.

"So?"

"So, we believe whoever attacked Maryjo was staying on this floor."

"And? What do you think you're going to find? Like a diary that says *I killed Violet and then did a bad job of strangling Maryjo. Must work on hand strength*?"

Percy narrowed his eyes at Mitch. "Or maybe a fictionalized version of events. Like, say, a novel."

"It's *true crime*," Mitch corrected.

"Whatever," said Percy. "Maybe Violet found out what you were doing, spying on her, faking—"

"*Faking* is an awfully strong word," Mitch interrupted. "I already told you, I'm a true Gatsby Leaguer. And I adored Violet. Just ... the whole story got a lot bigger after she turned up dead, didn't it? It could be a huge break for me."

I crossed my arms. "So you admit you're going to benefit from her death."

Mitch looked at Percy and jerked his head sideways, toward me, as if to say *Can you believe this woman?* "I might be able to make some lemonade out of lemons, but that's all it is. I didn't kill her. Obviously. What kind of writer puts himself in the story?"

"A stupid one," said Percy, at the same time I said, "An arrogant one."

"You know, you guys really need to be nicer to me." Mitch raised the gun again, if only a little. "We're partners now."

Chapter Twenty

BEFORE WE COULD LEAVE Mitch's room, I set off a whole new argument by saying I had to go downstairs. I pointed out, quite reasonably I thought, that it would look suspicious if nobody saw me for the whole dinner, and also that somebody had to gauge how much time we had left. But Mitch wasn't having it.

"How do I know you'll come back?" he wanted to know. "How do I know you won't go straight to the security guards? Or go down and tell everyone I'm holding you hostage at gunpoint?"

I blinked at him. "The whole reason we're bringing you with us is so you won't go down and tell everybody what's going on. Why would I go down and tell everybody what's going on?"

Mitch raised the gun, then stretched his arm out straight for good measure—directly toward me. "*This* is the reason you're bringing me."

He stepped forward. I'd been doing so well, but his

movements were too sudden, too quick. My chest tightened.

Plant growled. Percy got between us again.

Gun.

My stomach lurched. My mouth went dry.

Gun. Gun gun gun gun.

I silently counted to three, breathing deeply, and pushed down the panic that rose unbidden at the sight of anybody pointing a gun at me—even somebody I knew wasn't going to shoot it. I reminded myself of that second part again, and then once more.

"Yes, yes, you're a very scary villain." I was pleased to hear that my voice was just as calm and patronizing as I'd intended it to be. "Fine, I'll leave Plant with you. And Percy will be with you, anyway. I'm obviously not going to abandon them."

I looked at Percy. "Unless you want to do it the other way around, and you go downstairs?"

Percy snorted. "As if I'd leave you here alone with him."

"Why not?" Mitch sounded amused. "You claim to be so sure I won't shoot anyone."

"Yes, but you're freaking her out, waving that thing around."

"I did not *wave* it," Mitch protested.

Percy ignored him and looked back at me, his brow creased and his eyes soft with worry. "I assume you're freaked out?"

"Yeah." I held up my thumb and forefinger, about an inch apart. "A little. But I know as well as you do that he really won't shoot anybody."

Mitch gave me, and then Percy, a mutinous look. "Who says I won't?"

"Oh, come on," I said. "You're not allowed to profit off your crimes." I glanced at Percy. "Isn't that a thing?"

"Pretty sure it is," he agreed.

I turned back to Mitch. "You couldn't write your book at all, if the story ended with you shooting us."

"They wouldn't necessarily know it was me," said Mitch. "I could pin it on whoever we figure killed Violet."

"Let's review," said Percy. "You've got two security guards who would be here within seconds of a gunshot. And several more who would be here shortly after that."

Mitch pursed his lips. "If you're so sure I won't shoot you, why would you be freaked out?"

I sighed. "I've been a victim of gun violence."

"Twice," Percy added.

"I almost died the first time." I crossed my arms. "And I was doing really well with your gun, until you waved it directly at me."

Mitch threw back his head and made a drawn-out *ugh* noise. "*I did not wave it.* I know how to handle a gun. Only amateurs wave them."

"So you're not an amateur, then?" Percy asked. "You're a professional gunfighter? Pretty sure Doc Holliday is a different LARP."

"I've taken a couple classes." Mitch's tone had a definite defensive note to it.

I swallowed a laugh, and the last of my fear along with it. "So I'll meet you in Frank and Goldie's room, then?"

"Fine," said Mitch. "Do like a shave-and-a-haircut knock, so we know it's you."

"A secret knock? What are we, twelve?" I knelt down in front of Plant and gave him a kiss on the head. "Stay with Percy. I'll be back."

Percy smacked his thigh, and Plant went to stand beside him. I looked back at the two of them as I left the room—and was shockingly calm about it, all things considered. That wave of panic had been a reflexive response, and nothing more. No conscious part of me actually viewed Mitch as a threat.

Downstairs, I found Clarice standing at the front of the room by the piano, telling what seemed to be a very complicated story involving her, Violet, and a sailing outing gone wrong. I guessed it was funny, because everybody was laughing. Even Goldie and Ray, at the same time.

Perfect. Thoroughly distracted was just how I wanted my guests tonight.

But they were starting the fourth course. Of five. There would be drinks after dessert, too, but still. We needed to hurry.

I found the restaurant manager again. "No drama?"

She shook her head. "None that I've heard."

"Great. And sorry for abandoning you. We've got an unrelated emergency that we're dealing with. I'll probably be in and out."

She shrugged this off, looking slightly offended. "I've managed a dinner service or two in my time. We're fine."

I thanked her and headed back upstairs, where I did indeed do the shave-and-a-haircut knock on Frank and

Goldie's door. Percy opened it and waved me in, then closed the door behind me just as quickly. Honestly, we looked guilty as sin.

"Find anything?" I asked as I greeted Plant, who was wiggling like I'd been gone for fifteen days rather than fifteen minutes.

"Nope," Percy said.

I frowned at the scene before me: Mitch sitting on the floor, half inside the closet. It looked like Percy had been going through the bathroom, which was right next to the door. "You could've jumped him while his back was turned and taken the gun," I whispered.

"Sure, if I were an action hero," Percy whispered back. "But what would be the point in that? What am I going to do with the gun?"

"I don't know, make him go away?"

"I can hear you, you know." Mitch tossed a few shoes out of the closet, I guessed to search behind them. "There's nothing in here."

"Nothing in the bathroom, either," said Percy. "We still have the nightstands to check, and a couple of suitcases."

Mitch had insisted (in tantrum tones, if I'm honest) that we not wear gloves, if he didn't have any, so I got to work without further ado. I even went so far as to turn on Frank's e-reader and flip through the recently opened books, but there was nothing titled *Poisoning and Strangling for Nitwits*.

When that failed, I went to the other nightstand and picked up the first of two framed pictures Goldie had put there, next to a prescription bottle (allergy medication) and a glass.

It was a not-even-remotely-controversial photograph of her, Frank, and two girls who were clearly their daughters. "Is it weird she brought pictures with her?"

"Nah," said Percy. "A lot of people do that, especially for a long stay like this. Look." He opened the dresser drawer to reveal a row of neatly folded feminine clothes. "She's fully unpacked, too. She clearly likes things to feel like home."

I put the picture back and picked up the second one, smaller than the first. My heart broke a little bit as I studied it. "Maybe that's because her home was broken so early."

This photo, like the last one, showed a family of four: two parents and two young daughters. The mother was painfully thin. I recognized Danny Kilkelly from the newspaper articles I'd seen; this might even have been the same photograph they'd pulled from. He was smiling broadly, although there was something a little strained in it. Which I guessed wasn't surprising, considering his wife was clearly already ill.

Had he known how soon she was going to die?

Neither Violet nor Goldie looked like they knew. Their wide grins gave no evidence of a single care.

Was this the last happy memory Goldie had of her childhood? Was that why she brought it around with her?

I shook my head at my fanciful thoughts. She'd come from a close family, and her parents had died young.

What further explanation did I need, for a woman traveling with their picture?

The photographs told us nothing—much like the rest of the room. We left no stone (or pillow) unturned, but there was no comb. We'd hit a dead end.

"You know, Mitch," I said, as I zipped the final suitcase. It was empty—it must have held the clothes Goldie had unpacked. "You really ought to let us finish searching your room. If you've really got nothing to hide, why n— Plant! Leave it!"

I'd turned around to find Plant happily snuffling through the shoes Mitch had left in a heap outside the closet. "You big bonehead, if you left any teeth marks on those ..."

I grabbed his collar and snatched a plum-colored, three-strap pump out of his slobbery jaws. I recognized it from Goldie's costume that first night; the three straps had been noticeable.

I wiped it off with a scowl, first at Plant, then at Mitch. "I hope she didn't have these in a special order. You should have pulled them out and put them back one pair at a time."

Mitch rolled his eyes. "Who pays attention to the order of their shoes?"

"Lots of people." Percy came over to help me— mostly by keeping Plant occupied so the latter couldn't interfere.

Mitch waved a hand at the pile of shoes. "The twenties-looking ones, for her costumes, were at the back by the ironing board."

I flipped over the pump I still held, checking for any

damage that might be more permanent than drool. "So these are your fizzing investigative skills at work, I guess —" I stopped abruptly, staring at the shoe.

There was something stuck to the bottom. I pried it loose, as gently as I could, not wanting to rip it.

Percy squinted at it. "What's that?"

I stood and held it up to the lamplight. It was a flat, white, totally innocuous-looking cardboard disc, about the size of my thumbnail. The smooth roundness of its edge was broken in one spot by the tiniest of tabs. One side—the one that had been stuck to the bottom of Goldie's shoe—was faintly stained light brown.

That was when everything hit me.

And I mean all of it.

My mind played out a disjointed reel, like a montage in a movie. Allegra and Aaron, giving fever medicine to their baby. The bag from the drug store. Medicine they'd just bought.

The covers of Violet's books: Jack the Ripper, D. B. Cooper.

Goldie, telling me that Violet had been nagging her to join the league and come to the LARP for years. But this was the first year she'd given in.

Telling me that Violet was the reason their father wouldn't let them get a dog.

"Were the police ever in this room?" I asked. "How could they have missed this?"

"Missed what?" asked Percy. "What is it?"

"Well, easily," I said, "since they would have been looking for poison or whatever, and not at costume shoes that as far as they knew nobody was wearing when a crime was committed." Plant had come over to sit beside me, and was now looking up at me with his goofy canine smile, as if he expected me to hand over this prize that, really, *he* had found. I reached down to scratch his head. "And since they didn't have a nitwit dog to clean up after."

"But what *is* it?" asked Mitch.

I pulled out my phone and quickly scrolled through the album Goldie had sent me, of the pictures she'd taken at that first dinner.

It was all the confirmation I needed.

"Percy," I said softly, "call Ruby, will you? Ask if she can get out here right away."

Percy raised his brows. "Mind letting us in on what we need her for?"

"Because we've got some criminals in our dining room." I smiled slowly. "And we're about to get them to confess."

Chapter Twenty-One

STAN WAS at the front of the dining room, droning on and on about who cared what, and quite obviously did not appreciate my stealing his thunder.

"I'm sorry, Stan, but this can't wait." I turned to face the others, most of whom had finished their desserts and moved on to port and Irish coffee. I'd gotten down here just in time.

And I'd brought Plant with me. Restaurant or no restaurant, I figured he deserved his moment in the spotlight. I'd never have noticed that shoe if it weren't for him.

Percy was out in the hall, talking to Ruby, but Mitch had scurried in at my heels. Which I supposed was fair; I'd never have noticed that shoe if he hadn't left all the shoes in a pile like the nitwit he was, either.

"Since this is Violet's memorial," I said, "I thought you would all appreciate knowing who killed her. Ruby is on her way to arrest them as we speak."

Sort of. I hoped.

The guests started whispering and murmuring to each other. All except Mitch, who had no problem shouting at a completely unnecessary volume, for a group this small. He even cupped his hands around his mouth. "Stasia and Ray, right? Because upstairs you said 'criminals,' like plural. So that would have to be Stasia and Ray."

I tried not to laugh at him, unintentional clown that he was. I had declined to share anything with him on the way downstairs. And not just because he'd threatened me with a gun, either. I'm not super proud to admit this, considering one person was dead and another was in the hospital, which were obviously very serious things, but I was kind of looking forward to my Poirot moment.

And I was going to get it, because this really was like a Christie novel. Here they were, every suspect in Violet's murder and Maryjo's attack, all gathered in one room. Staring at me. With varying degrees of curiosity, impatience, and annoyance.

The impatience was the main reason I had to draw this out like an old-timey detective. Despite the urgency I'd conveyed to Stan, what I really needed to do was stall. Long enough for my plan to work. And long enough for Ruby to get here and witness it working, assuming Percy was persuasive enough to start her on her way.

I met Stasia's wide-eyed stare and shook my head. "No, I do not mean Ray and Stasia." I glanced at Mitch. "When I said criminals, I meant that one committed the murder, and the other the assault. But there's only one person responsible for Violet's death—"

"Well, obviously," Stan cut in. He was still standing

beside me, looking disgruntled. "If one did the murder and another the assault, it follows that Maryjo committed the murder, and was assaulted for it." He shook his head. "But I think you girls have it wrong, you and your police chief. Maryjo—"

"And that person is in this room," I finished, loudly enough to drown out the stansplaining. "Why don't you have a seat, Stan?"

He didn't, of course. Just crossed his arms and turned to face the others, so he was shoulder to shoulder with me. Like this was some sort of joint effort.

"Well, this is quite a lot of drama," Stasia said. "Suppose you tell us what you mean?"

I pointed at her. "You've been asking all along why you would have given the almond flavoring to the police, if you'd poisoned it yourself. It's a good question, but an even better one is why you would put the poison in the flavoring at all, when you had ready access to Violet's tea that day? Why not just poison the tea directly?"

I looked around the room. Still some impatience. Still some annoyance. But most of them seemed to be coming around. My promise that Ruby was coming was probably the reason for that; they probably all thought my little speech here was officially sanctioned.

"Because Violet would have seen her put it in the tea," said Mitch.

I shook my head. *Nitwit.* "Of course she wouldn't have. She didn't see Stasia put the flavoring in there, did she?"

Stan scoffed. "You'd have to be an idiot to carry poison in your purse on the day you planned to poison somebody with it. Not to mention that it was probably powder, which would have taken longer to mix—"

"All true," I said over him. "And I thought the same. But then it occurred to me that you would also need to use the flavoring to deliver the poison if you didn't know when, or whether, *you'd* be able to get to something Violet was eating or drinking—but you knew for sure that *Stasia* was going to get to something she was eating or drinking, at some point. So all you had to do was put the poison in the flavoring, and bide your time."

Percy walked into the room and came to stand beside me, on the opposite side from Stan, so that they flanked me like a couple of bouncers. Plant had been sitting next to me too, but as we were being very boring, he took this opportunity to lie on Percy's feet instead.

Without moving his lips, Percy whispered, "On her way."

She couldn't be long, then; it wasn't a long drive. I went on talking—and stalling. "It was a nice bonus, of course, that the fake-poisoner would be Stasia. The real poisoner knew she and Ray were involved with one another. They were the perfect pair to frame."

Stasia looked around, nostrils flaring, but there was no heated denial of an affair with Ray this time. It seemed she was more mad about being framed for murder. "A few of you knew what I was going to do with the flavoring."

"Yes," I said, "but only one had a chance to put cyanide in the bottle. There was a short window of time when the flavoring wasn't in your possession: while you were at dinner, the first night here. You went to bed early, if you recall, claiming a headache. Although to be honest, if we're confessing secrets, I think it was more because you were upset to see Ray being possessive of Violet, with Mitch here."

Stasia started to protest, but Goldie was louder.

"Nobody had a chance to poison it," she said. "It was a brand new bottle. She opened it herself, right before she used it. We all saw the bag, the box, the receipt."

"We did see those things," I agreed. "But we didn't see everything." I rubbed my thumb over the little cardboard disc I still held hidden in my hand. Such a thin, flimsy thing to be counting on for so much. "Somebody took advantage of that window of time. They slipped Stasia's room key out of her bag, went upstairs, and poisoned the flavoring. Then they put the bottle back in the box, and the bag, with the receipt. Probably the box was taped shut with one of those little tape circles; if they were careful enough when they pulled it off, they could have put that back on, too, preserving the illusion that the bottle was new."

I looked back at Goldie. "I never noticed you leave the dining room. But I saw you coming back, supposedly from the ladies' room, while I was in the hallway with Percy. Which means you had to have left dinner before I got out there. You'd have been gone a while. I don't know if you realized it at the time, but it was a huge stroke of luck for you when Stasia switched to a second-floor room. You were able to use the one staircase that didn't have a camera."

Without waiting for a response, I pulled out my phone and held it up, even though I knew nobody would really be able to see the screen from their seats. "You're the one who took this picture," I said to Goldie, "so you're not in it. But Stasia is in it, and that's your feathered headband by her elbow. You were sitting next to her. And the catch on her handbag was loose; we know that because it broke that same evening. You could have reached into that bag pretty easily to take her key, and then again to put it back."

Goldie huffed. "This is preposterous. What a convoluted explanation for how cyanide got into a bottle that *only Stasia is known to have handled*. Were my prints on the bottle?"

"A bottle's easy to wipe off," I said with a shrug. "But you're right; it is convoluted. Too convoluted to believe, maybe, except I found this."

The disc's turn had come. I held it up between my thumb and forefinger. Several people squinted, then whispered to one another that I was holding a very anticlimactic piece of paper or cardboard.

"It's a safety seal," I said.

"The kind that goes over the top of a bottle," Stan added. "You pull it off the first time you open it."

Thank you, Stan, because none of these folks have ever opened a bottle.

I nodded at Stasia. "You shook out the bag that day, for Roark, to show him you had just opened it. We all saw the receipt, the box." I held the seal a little higher. "But we didn't see one of these. There isn't one in evidence with that other stuff." At least, I assumed there wasn't. "Was the safety seal on the bottle when you opened it?"

"I ..." Stasia cocked her head and closed her eyes.

"I don't think so," she said slowly. "I think I just opened the cap and poured it. It never occurred to me." She shook her head, first at Ray, then at me. "But I couldn't swear to it. I didn't think about it at the time."

"You say you found that one," Goldie snapped. "Where, exactly?"

"In your room," I said. "On the bottom of one of the shoes you were wearing your first night here—the night in question."

"You were in our room?" Frank had been sitting quietly this whole while, but now he stood, looking outraged. Which suited me just fine. "You aren't allowed to go in our room!"

"Actually, we are. My dog smelled smoke, and alerted me to the problem."

I gestured at Percy for confirmation. He nodded and said, "Hotel staff is permitted to enter your room if they have reason to believe that you're engaged in illegal activity, or that you pose a danger to other guests. This qualified as both. If something hadn't been put out all the way, that's a fire hazard, and we generally like to get to those before the sprinklers start sprinkling."

"Put out?" Stan asked. "So you're talking about cigarette smoke?" He looked at me and shook his head. "Smoking isn't illegal. It might be against your rules, but that's not the same thing."

"It was a special kind of smoke," I said, then stansplained right back at him. "The kind that comes from a special kind of cigarette. The illegal kind."

Yep, that definitely sounded ridiculous. But no

matter. We didn't need anybody to actually believe it. All we needed was for it to be just plausible enough that Ruby wouldn't charge us with anything.

That might get us out of trouble, but I doubted it would make the safety seal admissible evidence. All of our "evidence," in fact, was either illegally obtained, or pure (in some cases wild) conjecture. Unless Maryjo woke up and corroborated our story, the only way the DA was going to get a conviction was if the police got a confession.

Which was why I was counting on Frank.

Frank, who detested a scene. Frank, who got flustered when he was the center of attention.

Every eye was certainly on him now. And he was every bit as flustered as I'd hoped.

"But you ... we didn't ..." he blustered. "And even if that was true, it doesn't give you the right to search our whole room!"

"I wasn't searching," I assured him. "I just happened to notice the shoe. It was on the floor next to the closet." I left off the part where Mitch was the one who'd tossed it there. And also the part where Mitch, who was definitely not hotel staff, was in their room at all.

"Sit down, Frank." Goldie sounded bored. I guessed she was a better actress than I'd originally given her credit for. "That's a scrap of paper. She's fishing. She's just trying to get you to incriminate yourself."

She was right, but I couldn't let that stop me. "Not only himself," I said. "Mostly you."

"Me."

"Of course." I looked her dead in the eye, making

sure I sounded as certain as I actually was (even if I totally couldn't prove it). "You killed your sister."

Goldie tossed her hands. "And why would I do that? Everyone knows how much I loved Violet."

"I'm guessing you loved your father more."

Now Goldie froze. She looked like I'd slapped her. I actually felt a little bad; it wasn't like she'd killed a good person, after all.

But then I remembered poor Maryjo, who wasn't technically a good person either, what with all the theft, but who didn't deserve what she'd gotten.

"And Violet killed him," I went on.

"Violet killed him!" Mitch shouted, with the air of somebody remembering the answer to a game-show question a second after the contestant already answered it. "Of course she did!"

"Of course she did," Goldie repeated. She snorted, I guessed just in case we'd missed the sarcasm dripping off her words. "And she did this because ...?"

"Money. She ..." I was momentarily distracted by the presence of Ruby by the wall near the door. How long had she been there? How much had she heard?

Enough that her hands were on her hips. Enough that her glasses were as low on her nose as they could go without falling off. Enough that she was looking pretty murderous herself.

But she hadn't interrupted me. Maybe she knew as well as I did that this way was best; I could say and do things up here that a cop never could.

Like lie. Just as an example.

I cleared my throat and looked back at Goldie.

"Doesn't it always come down to money? Violet got a lot of it, when your father died. As did you. But also because I think she was maybe kind of a sociopath? I don't know, you tell me, but there are things that point in that direction. She was charming, enchanting even, but never quite warm. She couldn't be trusted with a dog. She was very into how smart she was. And very into so-called perfect crimes. I think she copied Leopold and Loeb because she wanted to prove she could do it right."

"This is absurd," Goldie muttered.

"Was it because you finally agreed to do the LARP, so you were researching the twenties a bit?" I asked. "Especially organized crimes, famous crimes, that kind of thing, since you guys were doing a crime story. Is that how you came across the murder of Bobby Franks, and put it all together? Realized, after all this time, that it was Violet who took your father from you?" I cocked my head at her. "It's not *always* about money, is it? Sometimes it's about revenge."

"Absurd," Goldie said again, louder this time. "This is nothing but a story you made up. You'd make quite a LARPer, actually. But you haven't got a shred of proof or evidence for any of it. And no, a little piece of stolen garbage doesn't count."

I jerked my chin at Ruby. "Maybe you didn't see Chief Walker come in. I believe she's about to tell you all that Maryjo is awake, and is being interviewed as we speak. Do you suppose Maryjo has any evidence?"

It was kind of a ratbag thing, using poor Maryjo for manipulation. But I was doing it to get justice for her. And besides, I couldn't afford to feel guilty. I couldn't afford to let the confidence in my face (or the confidence I fervently hoped was in my face) crack even the littlest bit.

Because we were coming to it, now. The moment where my plan would either succeed, or magnificently fail.

I looked at Frank and raised my brows. "What do you think, Frank? Since it was you who tried to kill her?"

I did not know this, of course. Either Frank or Goldie could have done it. But given the physical nature of the attack, and their relative sizes, I was rolling the dice on Frank.

"Nice job that you didn't manage it, by the way," I went on. "Imagine what it would be like for your girls if both parents went away for murder."

Frank looked like he might vomit onto the remnants of his bourbon pecan pie. (Which looked really good. Success or magnificent failure, I should really either reward or comfort myself with some of that pie, after.) He'd sat down again, when Goldie told him to, and had been looking very steadfastly at the table.

But now he shifted sideways in his seat, an angle from which he could see just about everybody. His eyes darted around the room—at all the eyes that were on him. Nobody said a word, not even Ray. But their faces said plenty.

If anything could make Frank crack, I was pretty sure it was the collective judgment of the Carolinas Gatsby League.

"I guess she found out somehow, huh?" I pressed.

"And that's why you tried to shut her up?" I put on a shocked face. "Was she *blackmailing* you?"

He mumbled something.

"What's that, Frank?" I asked—or sort of yelled, really. If I could've put a spotlight on the man, I would have. "I didn't catch that."

But Goldie had caught it. "What is *wrong* with you, Frank?" she railed. "Get it together."

And then, for heaven and all the saints and every last LARPer to witness, the woman leaned across the table, and slapped her husband across the face.

All right then. *That* was definitely enough to make him crack. Or snap, more like.

He jumped out of his seat, looking furious and humiliated and hysterical and a little bit like a toddler who was about to have a breakdown.

"I said she was just trying to give that stupid comb back!" Frank screeched. He looked at me, then whirled around to look at Ruby. "I don't think she actually meant to spy. She just … I think she genuinely felt bad about the comb, after Goldie talked about it. She wanted to leave it outside our door, or something. Except she overheard us fighting, and we knew she overheard us fighting, because we heard her out in the hall."

Poor Frank was hit with the full force of Ruby's glasses. Honestly, it was probably worse than being hit with the full force of his wife's hand.

"So you …?" Ruby made a rolling gesture with her hand.

"I protected my wife." Frank straightened his spine,

fists clenched. "I protected my family. I hated to do it, but I didn't ... I couldn't ..."

And just like that, he crumpled again. He covered his face with his hands.

It was time to drive this thing home.

"What were you and Goldie arguing about, Frank?" I asked. "What did Maryjo hear?"

Without moving his hands, he said in a thick voice, "I'd just found out she killed her sister."

Chapter Twenty-Two

As it turned out, I hadn't lied (much): Maryjo really had regained consciousness. By the time the first course of Violet's memorial dinner was served, she'd already spoken to a police officer.

And told him she remembered absolutely nothing about the assault. She remembered nothing, in fact, since arriving at the LARP. She had to be told all over again about Violet's death. I heard she took it pretty hard.

Brain injuries are a tricky thing, and unpredictable. Although I wasn't given any details, I understood that Maryjo had several challenges ahead, some of which there was hope of fully overcoming, with time. But there was a strong chance those memories were gone forever.

Which put Ruby in a more forgiving mood, where my shenanigans were concerned. If I hadn't gotten Frank to confess the way I did, she might never have gotten enough evidence for either him or Goldie to be charged.

Sure, I went a little over the top with it. But only because I knew that was the only way it would work, the only way to break Frank. And not even a little bit because I'd enjoyed my own little live-action role-play, starring me as the detective.

As for the comb, Frank admitted that he'd taken it from Maryjo and stowed it away in the family car. She'd had it in her hand when he caught her eavesdropping; he never knew about the other stolen items in her purse.

So the Kilkelly family heirloom was back with its rightful owner—although I doubted she'd be able to take it with her to prison.

The remaining members of the Gatsby League checked out the morning after Violet's dinner. Once again Plant and I stood outside and watched their cars roll up, this time so they could drive away. (Highlights: Percy was with us, and I wasn't wearing a sack.)

Ray and Stasia came out together.

"Thank you." Stasia gave me a hug while they waited for the valets to pull their cars around. Or Violet's car, in Ray's case. "It hasn't been the easiest week, but at least we can try to move forward now."

I glanced at Ray. "Together, I take it."

Stasia shrugged. "It wasn't entirely what you think. Our situation was … complicated. And it doesn't mean we didn't love Violet."

"*Violet* was complicated," Ray added, shaking first my hand, then Percy's. "We did love her. That may sound strange, after everything, and knowing what you know now, but we did. We'll miss her."

"Oh yes," Stasia agreed. "Very much."

Ray was right: it did sound strange. But I didn't say so, only wished them well as they went on their way.

"Still loyal to Violet," Percy said, shaking his head. "She really did have charisma, didn't she?"

I frowned at him. "Where do you get *loyal* from? They were cheating. Or planning to cheat. Wanting to cheat?" My eyes widened. "You don't think they had Violet's *consent* to cheat?"

"Whichever way," said Percy, "that's unfaithful, not disloyal."

"That's not the same thing?"

"I think there's a difference."

"Ohhh ... kay. Well, for the record, I'd prefer you to be both loyal and faithful."

"You got it. I'm just saying, staying loyal to Violet's memory through everything—not just their lack of faith but Violet's whole, you know, psycho thing—is kind of honorable. In a twisted and creepy kind of way."

I snorted. "As honorable as you can expect from humans, anyway."

"Minerva Biggs," Percy said, one dimple peeking out, "how cynical of you."

"Most people, then," I amended. "You, I expect your usual level of chivalry from."

He looked past me, toward the inn's entrance. "And from these two, none at all."

I turned to see Stan and Mitch coming out together. They seemed to be deep in conversation as they emerged into the sunlight, dragging their suitcases behind them.

"... you avoid adverbs," Stan was saying. "You know, if you focus on the mother, that would be a fresh angle that nobody's considered."

"But the mother died years before," said Mitch. "There wouldn't even be a story if it was focused on her."

Stan shrugged. "If you lack imagination, maybe. Who knows what kind of mother she was? Violet suffered some trauma as a little girl. Otherwise she wouldn't have become a sociopath."

"I'm ... not sure that's how it works," Mitch said.

They went on arguing over how best to tell the story of the Kilkelly family, until they got in their respective cars. They barely acknowledged me and Percy, although Mitch did give Plant a departing pat on the head. Plant lifted his lip in return.

"Good boy," I told him, as the men drove away.

"Well then." Percy wrapped his arms around me, pulling my back against his chest. "I guess that's it. The LARP is officially over."

"Finally." I sighed, thinking of my apartment, and my friends, and my real life. It all seemed sort of distant now. "It's been a really long week, huh?"

He kissed my ear. "It had its moments."

I looked back at him, brow raised. "Good or bad?"

"Both, I'd say."

"THAT'S the last of them, I think." Snick heaved a long-suffering sigh as he watched one of the valets drive off in the most recent BMW.

We were standing in front of Baird House, directing the arriving wedding guests down the path to the garden

—our polite way of telling them they weren't wanted inside the house yet.

Snick and I, on the other hand, still had plenty to do inside, including wrangling the bride and groom, and their respective parents, and the photographer, and I hoped not the minister, as he shouldn't require wrangling, but who could say, really. The ceremony was due to begin in precisely twelve minutes, and I prided myself on the punctuality of my events.

"I'm exhausted already," said Snick. "I woke up exhausted already."

I elbowed him. "Nevertheless, we must persevere."

We went inside and started toward the library, where Elaine and Mrs. B were closeted away in advance of their big entrance. But we didn't get very far before my phone vibrated in my hand. I tapped the screen to find a text from Dante, the Bairds' personal chef:

Your caterer is a moron. I am NOT serving the salad like this.

Dante wasn't one to mince words.

"I've got to go deal with a salad crisis," I began, but was interrupted by Percy and Tristan coming down the sweeping front staircase. Tristan called my name in his laughing-at-somebody-else's-drama voice. A bad sign.

"I'll handle the salad," said Snick. "You handle the brothers Baird."

"Your job sounds easier."

Snick snorted and went off toward the kitchen, just as Percy and Tristan cleared the bottom step. Percy looked considerably calmer than his brother. A good sign. He whistled at me as they approached.

"Look at you." His eyes swept up and down my simple cocktail dress.

I pursed my lips at him. "You just saw me twenty minutes ago. I looked exactly the same."

"True, but it takes my breath away every time."

I laughed. "Oh, you are good."

"I like to think so."

"I'm begging you. Please. Stop." Tristan pressed his fingers to his face, just below his eyes. "All this love hurts my sinuses. So. Phil's locked himself in the guest room—"

"He didn't lock it," said Percy.

"—and he's refusing to come out."

Percy rolled his eyes. "Don't mind the Drama Llama. He just said he isn't ready yet, and that we should tell you."

"No, that's not what he said." Tristan gave me a pointed look. "He said he needs to see you."

Okay, that was a horrible sign.

"And by the way, " Tristan went on, "he isn't even letting his parents in there. The *dogs* aren't even in there anymore."

I frowned. "Wait, where are the dogs?"

"Moved them to my room," Tristan said with a wave. "Plant's sound asleep under a blanket of Frenchies, he's fine."

Lucky Plant. Still. This was bad.

When a bride or groom asked to see the wedding planner—privately—this close to the ceremony, it almost always meant something had gone very wrong. I could only hope it was the boutonniere and not cold feet.

Except Phil wasn't the type to be picky about his boutonniere.

"He needs a best man to talk him down," said Tristan. "I *told* you they should've had a wedding party."

I made a vague *mm-hm* noise that could be interpreted as either confirmation or denial. I'd seen Tristan exactly once since Elaine got engaged, the day Violet Kilkelly died. He'd told me no such thing.

Now Percy looked worried, presumably because I did. I smiled and squeezed his hand. "It's all right. You guys just go outside and make sure people are sitting down, okay? And take your own seats, we're starting soon." *I hope.*

I hurried up the stairs, to the second-floor bedroom that had been designated for Phil's use. "Phil?" I called as I knocked. "It's Minerva."

He opened the door, pulled me inside by the elbow, then closed the door behind me, all in what felt like an instant. He looked ready, at least (and handsome, with his too-long-in-my-opinion black hair neatly tamed). But he was pacing. And there was a thin sheen of sweat on his forehead.

Bad signs.

"You're the only one I can talk to about this," he said. "You're the only one who will get it."

I blinked at him. That didn't sound like a wedding planner thing. It sounded like a friend thing, which was frankly bizarre. Not that Phil and I weren't friend*ly*. But I really only knew him as Plant's vet and Elaine's fiancé. I couldn't recall us having a single conversation where one or the other of them hadn't been present.

"Get what?" I asked.

I cringed as Phil ran a hand through his hair. So much for neatness. "I don't think even the Italian guy would get it." He stopped pacing and turned to face me. "But this is insane, right?"

"The wedding is insane?"

"No, the *Bairds* are insane."

I bit back a laugh. The poor guy wasn't wrong.

Phil sat down on the edge of the bed, elbows on his knees and head hung low. "Their whole lives are insane. They've got—we've got—an Oscar winner and two congressmen outside right now."

And one senator, I added, but only in my head. I had the sense it wouldn't be a terribly helpful comment.

"We were in New York a few weeks ago," Phil went on, "for this animal rescue benefit thing? And somebody took our picture. Like, a *paparazzi*." He looked up at me. "Elaine's got an ex-boyfriend with two *Grammys*. I'm a *vet*."

He was right: I did get it. I'd had similar thoughts of my own on more than one occasion. I sat next to him and gave his shoulder an awkward pat. "The Bairds are a lot. They come with a lot. But you love her. She's worth it."

Phil scrubbed a hand over his jaw. "I do love her. You know I'm not questioning that, right? Because I have zero cold feet when it comes to Elaine. Like not even a slight chill in one toe. But you marry a girl, her family becomes your family. And I knew that all along, obviously, but now that it's really here ... I think I might have cold feet when it comes to being part of the Baird machine."

"Look," I said, "I'm your wedding planner. Everything out there"—I gestured at the window—"is my job. If you need me to stall, I'll stall. If you need me to tell everybody to go home, I'll tell them to go home. But I don't think it would do you much good. It's too late, my friend."

Phil hung his head again, but he nodded at the same time. "You're right. I couldn't leave Elaine at the altar." He scoffed. "What am I even doing right now? I would never break her heart."

I shook my head. "I'm not talking about her heart, I'm talking about yours. I think in your heart, you're married to Elaine already. And that's the one place you can't get a divorce. Nothing that does or does not happen today is going to change it."

Phil looked at me like I'd just turned on a lightbulb over his head. "That's true. That is *exactly* true." He smiled. "And anyway, if you can be brave, I can be brave, right? It's so much worse for you. You're going to have to take the house."

I gave him a wary look. "What house?"

"*This* house, obviously. Baird House." He cocked his head. "What are you going to do with Mrs. B? Is she going to keep living here, after you're married?"

My laugh sounded almost as awkward as I felt. "Percy and I aren't engaged, Phil. We practically just started dating." It only felt longer, because the Carolinas Gatsby League's week-long LARP had lasted, by my count, approximately ninety-three years.

Phil waved this off. "Right, so you won't get married tomorrow. But of course you'll get married someday. Everybody can see you're endgame."

Everybody? Everybody who? Is Percy one of the everybody?

I let it go; this wasn't about me, and Phil was now officially late for his own wedding. "So what's the verdict?" I asked. "One way or another, I need to get downstairs. Are you coming, or not?"

"Coming." He stood and offered his hand to help me up. "Thank you."

"That's what I'm here for."

I opened the door—and nearly collided with Percy, who was standing there with his arm raised, like he was about to knock.

How long had he been out there? What had he heard?

"We ready?" he asked.

"We ... um ..." I knew he was talking about the wedding, but in light of that last bit of my conversation with Phil, it just felt like a loaded question. I chose to scowl instead of answering it. "What are you doing up here? You're not supposed to be in the house."

Percy offered me his arm, and there were those dimples that I suspected would never stop making my stomach flutter. "If you're here I'm here, right?"

Right.

Dear Reader

Thank you for reading *Past Resort*. I hope you enjoyed it! Minerva's next adventure is *The Guest is History*.

If you'd like to know when I've got a new book, be sure to sign up for my newsletter at cordeliarook.com. You'll find my email address there as well; I love to hear from readers!

Your honest ratings and reviews help other readers choose books. I hope you'll consider giving your opinion at your online retailer.

Minervaisms

butter upon bacon: even more of a good thing; over the top; an extravagance

carriwitchet: a befuddling question; a puzzle

fizzing: excellent; impressive

hornswaggle: a con; a willful deception

nanty-nark: have great fun; party

odsbodikins: an all-purpose expression of dismay, surprise, or irritation

pantry politicking: gossiping among the household, staff, or servants

podsnappery: a refusal to recognize the unpleasant; complacency

ratbag: a jerk; a sleazy person

Made in the USA
Columbia, SC
12 May 2023

16518009R00133